John T. Kinsella lives in Hertfordshire where he was born. One of his many interests include our 'Ocean Environment' and its species and in particular the Killer Whale, Orcinus orca. For many years John worked within the Offshore Oil and Gas Construction Industry on whose behalf he travelled, worked and lived in differing countries such as Ireland, Iran, Brazil, Qatar, Nigeria, America and Abu Dhabi; he has also travelled to many different parts of the World such as New Zealand, Canada, Norway, Sweden, France, Spain and Portugal among others. The travel stimulated an interest in life including man's preoccupation with discovery, a subject matter which intrigues him to this day.

For Nicholas and Kristin

John T. Kinsella

VOICES IN THE SEA

AUSTIN MACAULEY PUBLISHERS™

LONDON • CAMBRIDGE • NEW YORK • SHARJAH

A CIP catalogue record for this title is available from the British Library.

ISBN (9781788239974) (Paperback)
ISBN (9781788239981) (Hardback)
ISBN (9781788239998) (E-Book)

www.austinmacauley.com

First Published (2018)
Austin Macauley Publishers Ltd™
25 Canada Square
Canary Wharf
London
E14 5LQ

Chapter 1
The Shaman

"I, Chulyin, Shaman of the North, am the Peregrine, and I am flying upon the wind of time. At this very moment, my wings craft the wind, its waves of tumult throw me higher and higher, but this wind is not the wind of the African Savannahs; blown from the Gods sleek copper trumpets, nor is this wind of the Mongolian plains where the Gods brush the sharp tips of the long green grasses that whisper quietly like the willowy flute's most sympathetic notes. This wind is neither of the European gusts, that merrily dance up hill and down dale, whilst throwing up autumnal leaves in the silence of the glistening silver symbols final cascade. Nor is this an Arctic wind that sounds its blustering snowy chill, calling, always calling like the soft voices of one of the Gods choirs. This is the wind of the desert; sharp and vivid yet whipping and tumbling like the almost silent echo that follows a lasting beat of the drum. Beneath my outstretched wings, drums are sounding, as men divided by malevolent and egotistical quests for power not made of tradition, pray in unison to the words of a book of good yet some of these men are folding and turning and twisting the pages and words beyond the realms of their God's redemption; whilst further below and amidst the rubble of man's dominions; red blood rivulets of creation run thick and sticky from innocent man, woman and child alike leaving a raging flooding stream of the teacher's angry memories to quickly congeal in the wounded mentality of the newly born child. Behold, the sound of a soothing choral choir; there are protests, but the noise of conflict and war are drowning out this clarion call for peace, and all this is happening whilst one man and then another beat the same drums sounding out the echoing debates, that passionately claim jurisdiction over the minds of the Gods."

"I, Chulyin, Shaman of the North, know that the existence of all life depends on resolutions, and so I, once the Peregrine and now the Arctic Tern, fly again in the North and out to sea and beyond these raging angry scenes of death, and I watch as long grey boats of war thrust their way forward against the Gods currents and tides to honour promises that some may never keep. He hunts doth man, and yet mankind has always been obliged to hide; from predators, from weather and from each other and as distrust, born as it is from ignorance, endows itself with power, until power itself reaches onwards and upwards unto that threshold of a debacle which may herald the prospect of the final extinction of life. East and West are in conflict again, which may result in the war to end all wars and all of life, unless the Gods decide that I, Chulyin, Shaman of the North, should intervene. I do not lament for what would be the purpose in lament when I am aware that all of life is forever in the process of leaving, or staying whilst the spirits in the guise of beings, which only ever borrow the clothes of nature, continually arrive and depart, and as man's measurement of the hour, the minute and the second disappear into the rushing past, bringing forth a present and future, which are nothing more than more of times discarded moments. Alas, for those that wish to keep, for nothing that the spirit sheds, will the spirit have ever owned and only the creative moment will exist until second by second, life's experiences are cast into a past that was once the present. I must fly again on the wind of time, and I fly with no apprehension, for no two flights are the same, and no two actions are the same, and no two beings are the same nor thoughts are the same as of those that had preceded the former, and so it is that all living things follow the infinite reality of life."

"I, Chulyin, Shaman of the North, am the Peregrine again, and I soar above the jumbled ruins of the 'Temple of Zeus', and way beyond broken stones that were once fashioned by hardened hands that toiled with only the fertile imagination and tools of pride to pile high these stones and one above the other bringing forth the magnificent edifices of the city of Olympia. I ask myself, what has become of this 'Temple of Zeus'? But before I can ponder on this question further, I am thrown aside and amidst the wind of time and within a millionth of a second the Gods are allowing me to soar above the sumptuous and flowing green and frothed white tumbling River Alpheus and the sumptuous and flowing green and frothed white tumbling River Kladeos and above this ancient land of Greece where a man of noble birth, Solon, will in time wrestle with the idealistic to lay thick upon the mind of mankind the prospect of democracy, but now, I must watch as the Games have started in Olympia, and a first race has begun, in which proud and able-bodied men compete for the honour of wearing the 'Olive Green Wreathed Crown' which, in this time, is the universal symbol of peace. I soar way above this city of Olympia, and I watch closely with forty thousand or more excited and cheering souls from different dominions, who have come to encourage champions of political difference, but just and peaceful men of sinew muscle and bone, who all run fast in pace against the will of each other in ardent competition and in honour of their God Zeus, God of sky and thunder, God and King of all Gods, who watches over all proceedings that happen to occur, farther and wider than the blue red sky above which orbits all of earth's creation. Such is man at peace, but the ever-present rumblings of war make passage for new Kings to come and old Gods to disappear, leaving past homage to new wisdom and unto the annals and pages of disbelief. The wind of time is taking me back into the present; I go to look for more evidence of man at peaceful competition, and Zeus and I depart from each other's company, as we both travel in different directions in time. The wind of time is taking me to a time of consolidation, a time of peace, but again, it is the calm before the storm to come, as man once again demonstrates man's inhumanity to man."

"I, Chulyin, Shaman of the North, am on the wind of time. Now, I am the Raven and I am watching man again from above on soft and lighter airs at more peaceful competition below my outstretched wings, but yet again, I sense the rumblings of war and even here amongst the peoples of a peaceful nation. A boat race is beginning in a city named London, and I watch closely as one of man's ceremonial coins, a golden and British sovereign, spins in the air of a balmy Easter afternoon, and it spins like one of the God's silver planets and against the gravity of the Gods until its momentum falters, and it falls again unto the earth. The moon has moved again, and one of the God's flood tides has returned and begins to sweep up this river that man has named 'The Thames' and a fluttering and dignified umpire's bright red flag ceremoniously drops. Another race is beginning and multiple oars, held very firmly in already blistered and bound fingers and thumbs begin dipping silently in the water, seemingly trying to save seconds of time after time, and both boats of man's blues speed across the surface of the greyish-green Thames water below as if propelled by nothing more than an invisible wind, but each member of the blue boats crews are pulling lifting and pulling and lifting both port and starboard oars as if their lives are depending on the perfection that man will always strive to reach; the blades of the oars turning time and time again to the horizontal and then twisting perfectly towards the vertical before dipping beneath the surface of the greyish-green water again and again and again, and all of this motion installed in the minds of all in order to defeat the turbulence and spray of oncoming rushing air, wind and water. I fly lower and below the curtains of whispery cirrus clouds, and I watch as the oars continue without relapse, moving always to the horizontal and then back to the vertical, and I watch as all of the blades dip again and again and again and in near perfect motion beneath the surface of the water until both boats of men are inseparable over a stretch of water that man has named Fulham Reach, a Cambridge boat's crew just edging ahead with quicker intermittent bursts of propulsion and at a First Mile Post, and now, whilst approaching another stretch of water that man has named Crabtree Reach with a bridge named Hammersmith in sight, whilst an Oxford crew are veritably scything through the water, which man had has named the Middlesex side. They begin to pull harder on their oars, but the Cambridge boat with the advantage of a Surrey side edges half a length ahead; they are now edging, edging forwards, as if threatening to gain another length, and until yet another struggle with this Surrey Bend comes upon both boats of blues, and now the Cambridge boat pushes up again and are just, only just beyond a length in front, moving the Oxford coxswains voice to unleash across the greyish-green water, where it seems to stay for all the time in the world and in the ears and minds of the Oxford eight, who pull and strain to the beyond of the parabolic disadvantage of the Surrey Bend until finally edging closer and closer and closer still, until half a length has become less than the half a league or more that seemed to besiege them, and now in sight of a Barnes Bridge the two coxswains at sincerest war with each other, implore their boats of blues to propel forward with God's speed, for this is all the worth for man at peace, and I watch all of the desperate final exertions that pull and push, pull and push, pull and push unto a Mortlake finish line that touches the Oxford boat of blues first, releasing all of ecstasy and all of pain out across and up and down this River Thames and far and wide until installed in all environs of thought, leaving behind only the echoing memories of coxswains voices sounding out across the water and down amongst the blue boats hulls, reaching the ones that were eights, the eights that were ones, and all of this memory set in everlasting testaments to the given all. But now, I hear the promise of sound in the sky, breaking above me, and I must leave this realm of time to see a future's path and once again it is a path of destruction, where new Kings may come and old Gods may disappear and perhaps into the annals of yet more disbelief!"

"I, Chulyin, Shaman of the North, am once again upon the wind of time which has thrown me into one of the future's paths. Now the Raven, I have settled not too far away from the burnt and broken citadel of London and in a rich bushy thicket with plucky green leaves, but I do not feast upon the lush, moist, red and juicy berries that the God's golden photons had once brought to bloom for my palette, for they are covered in hot radioactive dust. I am forewarned of a deluge to come as I hear the pitter-patter of ever so soft raindrops, and I fly upwards beyond one sad quantum of solace towards another, where the Gods allow me to watch the billions and billions of glistening silver, grey and white raindrops form. I watch, as the millions become billions, and I watch closely and listen to the sound that are billions and more billions of pitter-pattering drops, as these molecules of hydrogen and oxygen fall to the earth below. I look even more closely, and as more torrential precipitation appears from the heavens; the rain of two hydrogen atoms and one oxygen atom all spitting and then smattering upon unsuspecting and saddened and scorched blades of once verdant grass until finally achieving the cascade. I watch as these molecules of water then spill over all of the high river banks, and I watch as the Gods rain begins its task of mastering all of the life that is left; I watch as harried and poisoned men struggle with their boats, and all this is happening whilst natures rippling muscles of the hydrogen and oxygen molecules wrestle with each other, for in the river I can see billions of molecules bound in unison, seemingly like writhing, seething and caressing anacondas, enthusing both old and the new life alike to leave or stay in the throw of a transitional tide, born of the plutonium that an enemy have secreted from the earth, and all of life that is left is left damaged and will remain so until the deluges cascade of cleansing reaches onwards in time to beyond the era and into the epoch and the aeon when all will be vibrant again. Beneath and above my outstretched wings are all manner of dusts and particles that rise up and continue to rise up and until they surround me on all sides; now I see neither close nor far and still these wind-blown remnants of the earth's crust rise further above to block out the Sun God's golden photons, from falling unto the earth, and yet there is no consequence, for nothing lies beneath; there are no green shoots of life to feed on the nutrients of the soil, for they have all been scraped away from the surface of the earth by man's fingers and thumbs, and man with only his mind and his hands is right now reaching down in reprisal towards the bowels of the earth, taking with them ore of iron, and ore of copper, and ore of aluminium and silvery white shards of silicon from the sands of time, and on land and sea, he searches for the death of life; carbon itself, and more of plutonium and all to make the technology with which man does hope to succeed in endeavours which he does not yet fully understand.

"I, Chulyin, Shaman of the North, can fly and swim, but such dexterity man does have, for he is the master of fire and flame that cuts the ore and shapes his metal to fit in the hand, and then he makes a trinket that he adorns his being with, then a wheel with which to make a cog and a cog with which to make a wheel, and then a furnace by which he melds his steel and then clocks with which to delay or accelerate the motions of his technologies, and yet, there can be no calibration that emulates that which the Gods have made in nature. Still I look and listen for the sound of nature's life but to no avail for all of beautiful life has gone from this place which was once full of the sound of running water, the bird and the deer."

"I, Chulyin, Shaman of the North, am on the wind of time again and I fly as the Raven. I am back in the city of London's present, and below my outstretched wings, I see tall, uniformed buildings of hardened grey concrete and glistening silvery glass reflecting the Sun's photons in splayed activity that momentarily blinds. The buildings stand in naive majesty on levelled streets and thoroughfares alongside artificial, bright yellow lights which sparkle and twinkle brightly in the late evening night air. I watch as deciduous saplings planted by man's hand, tremble in silent awe, as the weight of passing traffic moves earth asunder, and all of this is happening whilst the fertile space above and between land and sky waits patiently and in askance for all manner of green leaves to breathe in the spluttering traffics carbon dioxide, that hangs in the air like invisible and toxic street level cirrus. All of life begs for the promise that green deciduous leaves will bring, a promise which will bring forth a product of photosynthesis, oxygen itself, and into this city's environment, which can only beg for more and more whilst man made concretions continually strive to conquer the space which nature has reserved for itself. Yet time gives no quarter and only time decides which will be the victor or the vanquished, and time is on the side of nature that creeps ever forward and unto the preside of man who will forever try, and try again and again, to impose his will against the design of the Gods."

"I, Chulyin, Shaman of the North, look down below my outstretched wings again and see nature on the march, for the street lighting does not confound the nocturnal hunt of the quick red fox that arrogantly defies the logic of a conformity, which naively attempts to stifle evolution. I laugh inwardly as I watch the fox contemptuously trailing its long bushy tail across small stalks of uneven but graceful verdant grasses, which have emerged between the gaps of the grey and even paving slabs, and as if life is in proclamation of arrival amidst these plateaus of man's creative genius, and all found by photons and rain, photons and rain, photons and rain each arriving and falling, arriving and falling, arriving and falling upon the perfect designs of man. And time pays no homage to man's speed which is measured in the second, the minute, the hour, the day, the month and the year; for mother nature's attention is set firmly on the era, and the epoch, and aeon, all of which will inevitably defeat the efforts of man whilst reaching ever forward on to the resides of the new and embryonic species of life, and yet all is well with man in this present day, and all is well with man's peaceful struggle which will if uninterrupted and in the course of time come to equal terms with mother nature. Such is the will of the Gods."

"Time is the rhythm, to which we all must dance,
And time's song will continue on,
Unperturbed by a note that misses its beat,
Or by those that collude to disrupt its tune,
After all, the whole will always be greater than the sum of its parts,

Listen, I hear a sound,
Tap tap!
There, it is again,
Tap tap!
The Gods demand my attention,
A new symphony is about to begin!"

Chapter 2
Eleanor

Eleanor knew she had awoken at an unseemly hour, although, she quickly looked through the lilac shadowy curtains and out onto the veranda, just to see if there was any sign of life; there was, for it was almost daylight and although the sky was streaked with the differing coloured hues that signalled the break of day; these magentas and violets playing silent sonatas with her eyes in a cool light breeze. Peter, a Canadian photographer, whom they had been introduced to in Vancouver, had set the camera up perfectly; it was already switched on to the record button; he had developed this piece of innovative equipment. It had first and foremost been designed as an underwater camera and recorder with one important facet; it could slow down the recording to a fraction of the normal speed allowing for advanced scientific analysis. Eleanor was hoping to catch a glimpse of one or two of Vancouver's famous hummingbirds on her veranda which was lined with multicoloured flower pots and on the huge white screen that she had hung on the far wall in the living room. Excited at the prospect of getting the film recording she wanted, Eleanor rushed to the bathroom and immediately got into the shower. Within minutes she had soaped herself, rinsed off and was in the process of drying down when her mobile phone rang; she ran to the living room almost stumbling over the towel which had tangled between her legs and picked the phone up.

"Hello, Eleanor speaking."

"Good morning, Eleanor, I'm afraid that I have some bad news!"

"Oh no! Please don't tell me it's the installations!" Eleanor almost yelled.

The Professor had advocated the use of sophisticated installations which were to be immersed in the sea, and in order to attract the intelligence of Orca, the Killer Whale, the Professor believed that all previous attempts at communication were signifying to Orca that man was primitive, and that Orca's response was in kind. It was in Eleanor's opinion, a fair assessment, given the latest knowledge they had acquired on Orca intelligence, and so the team who had given themselves the task of translating the language of the cetacean had consulted and consorted with the very best artists and engineers in both the United Kingdom and Canada, when making each one.

The Professor paused for a second or two. "Now, now Eleanor, there is no need to be pessimistic; it's a minor hitch which means that delivery to the dockside will not be as planned, but we can expect to start tomorrow morning at first light."

"Have there been any sightings of any pods in the sound?" Eleanor enquired.

"Not yet, but I have been told that a pod has been sighted out near Vancouver Island, heading in our direction; don't worry, they'll be here. I hear plenty of salmon have reached the inlet!" The Professor replied emphatically.

"Do you want me to come over to you today, Professor?" Eleanor asked.

"No, that is not necessary, Eleanor," came the reply, and the Professor continued, "Take the time to enjoy yourself, go and see the sights, I understand that the Anthropology Museum is a must-see venue, why not take a trip over there?"

"That sounds like a good idea, would you like to come with me, Professor?" Eleanor asked.

"Oh, no thank you, Eleanor, I have a lot of preparatory work to do before tomorrow, you go on and enjoy yourself; I'll see you tomorrow morning!"

As per his wish, the Professor rung off abruptly, and before Eleanor could think further on the subject matter of their brief discussion, her eyes were accosted as the screen in front of her came to life.

*****

The hummingbird was beautiful and must have been merely inches long, despite the fact that its picture filled the screen; the resolution was perfect. Eleanor calculated that its wings were probably moving at about fifty beats per second, although the camera recorder had slowed down the oscillation to a mere fraction of that speed. The colouring absolutely astounded her; it had a bright shiny emerald green back and ruby red throat; there were grey flanks and a forked tail which seemed to be stifling any unbalanced movement. Quickly she reached for her book on North American birds which lay with the guide to Vancouver on the rather cluttered coffee table, but before she could open the book, the hummingbird had gone. Somewhat disappointed, Eleanor switched off the camera and went into the kitchen to make a cup of coffee, resolving to watch the recording that evening. Eleanor, although a specialist in Marine Biology, found interest in all matters related to ecology. Postponing the referencing of the hummingbird, she reached for her guide to Vancouver instead and just as the coffee percolator sprung into life. Eleanor flicked through the pages of the guide to look for the Museum of Anthropology; she decided that she would go there after she had taken breakfast.

Eleanor found a breakfast bar not far from her apartment; it was French; although, the proprietor and waiting staff were all Canadian. It was named 'Le Petit Château', and it lay quietly off the precipice of a boulevard close to Granville Bridge. It was an ideal place where she could sit and take in the sights and sounds of Vancouver as the city came awake; not that Vancouver ever really slept; it was always a busy place. Eleanor was, however, taking her time this morning and whilst tucking into her traditional English breakfast, she even had time to strike up a conversation with a gentleman who had asked her if she had a light of all things; she hadn't, being a non-smoker, but he remarked on the ambience of 'Le Petit Château', and she had to agree; conversation followed on from there. Eleanor wasn't used to talking about her work but the gentleman, following no professional protocol, had by good manners, obliged her to reply. She found herself talking in some detail about her work, which the Professor had advised her not to do and even whilst talking, she mentally chastised herself. The gentleman, who she thought was Canadian, seemed interested, and Eleanor came very close to expositions that Eleanor did not want to reveal, but it was all up to but not touching sensitive areas, at least most of it was. Eleanor had been given a few tips on sailing in English Bay, having discussed the previous day's itinerary. Despite the conviviality, however, Eleanor resolved not to talk about the installations to anyone outside the team again, and when they had finished their coffees the young man, who sat on the table next to Eleanor's, looked worriedly at his wristwatch and left his table rather hurriedly, only looking behind him to wave goodbye. Eleanor was unaware that a recording instrument hidden from view and not two blocks away had been listening to every word that she had to say.

*****

The first thing that struck Eleanor was the very image of the museum; the entrance was a tiered structure of one white parapet succeeded by other white parapets in height; it was flanked by tall, evergreen trees and stood as a testimony to good architecture all set before rippling running water that sailed past green and white lily pads; rushes of different kinds lined the banks. There was a bronze statue of a 'Breaching Orca', emblazoned with abstract designs right outside the museum. Mesmerised by the design, Eleanor stood there for a while taking in the sights and sounds of the park and decided to photograph the statue, not realising that she was the first visitor that day and was being watched by a curator who was, right at that juncture, opening the doors of the museum. Eleanor took her photographs and walked slowly towards the door; the man greeted her.

"Good morning, Madam, I see that we have another lovely day, welcome!"

"Good morning," Eleanor replied, smiling broadly at the man who was attired in a smart blue suit and matching tie. She noticed his name badge, which denoted that he was of native descent.

"I'm not sure what I've come to look for, but I was advised to visit the museum. I have an interest in anthropology and all other life for that matter." Eleanor continued to smile at the man.

"Are you British?" the curator asked her immediately.

"Yes, I am," Eleanor replied.

"Oh, you are on vacation then!"

"Well, not exactly, I'm here to study the Orca's in and around Vancouver Island," Eleanor replied, still not being able to stop herself; such was her enthusiasm for her work.

The curator stopped shuffling the pamphlets that he had in his hand to give her and regarded her for a moment.

"Orca?"

"Yes, 'Orcinus orca', the Killer Whale, I'm a scientist, and I am with a team who are embarking upon a programme of study. Our aim is to start the process of translating its language," Eleanor replied.

The minute she spoke, Eleanor seemed to realise yet again that she shouldn't be talking about the work that they all had to do, but it was no matter, for the man was apparently oblivious to the words that seemed to Eleanor to pour out of her mouth, indeed much to her satisfaction, he did not question her further on the subject. However, the curator began to stare at her again which almost put her ill at ease, until she mused that it was just his demeanour that was different and probably due to his differing culture.

"Would you like a tour? We could take in some of the Inuit artefacts, part of our belief is that Orca was mankind's ancestor and that we came from the sea as well!" Eleanor jumped at the chance.

"Really, well that is interesting and the answer to that offer is yes, yes that would be wonderful! Are you Inuit then?"

"I am!" he rather proudly announced and started walking toward some exhibits.

The man kept looking at Eleanor whilst handing her the pamphlets which he had previously been organising. They then both walked side by side as the curator went from one exhibition to another pointing out the significant artefacts which each had in its display; he only stopped to explain the rudiments of fashion and ritual of each piece that captured Eleanor's interest. As they walked, the curator politely questioned Eleanor about her home in the United Kingdom. Eleanor responded with descriptions and anecdotes which held the curators interest, but she did not elucidate any further on the work that they were embarking on. They ventured past artefacts which were thousands of years old, some of which bore testimony to the beliefs of mankind throughout history, and Eleanor asked what must have seemed a thousand questions, all of which were answered by her guide whose competency and intelligence was quite evident. The minutes passed by into the hour until the time came for Eleanor to interrupt the tour.

"I'm afraid I simply must go and get something to drink, perhaps, I can come back another time, thank you so much for showing me around."

"Oh, but I haven't shown you the Inuit artefacts; they are not on display at present; let me take you quickly downstairs to our archive room," the curator replied sounding a little anxious.

"I should think that will be alright providing it doesn't take too long," Eleanor replied.

Eleanor followed the curator down to an adjacent staircase and along an echoing and eerie corridor which led to a tall black door. The curator stopped before it, retrieved a bunch of keys from his jacket pocket and opened the door for Eleanor. It was dark beyond this threshold and Eleanor felt momentarily frightened until the curator's hand switched on the wall and ceiling lights. Eleanor was then confronted by row upon row of what appeared to be silver metal or aluminium archive cabinets; the room was full of them. Eleanor was led around the tall cabinets until they reached the cabinet which read 'Inuit Artefacts.' The curator just stood there saying nothing for about five minutes or more until Eleanor asked a question.

"What were the drum and the rattle used for?"

"Ahh, the drum and the rattle were used to help send the Shaman on his journeys," the curator replied.

"The Shaman? Oh, of course, they believed in Shamanism way back then, didn't they?"

The curator now stood fully erect before her; he seemed to tower over her.

"The Inuit, like so many other tribes, still believe in the Shaman, Madam! Shamanism is and always has been a major part of our beliefs!"

"Really?" Eleanor said, thinking that the way she replied might attract more information; she was however, unprepared for what came next.

"I know one! A Shaman, he is one of the most respected people in the Pacific Northwest. He's here in Vancouver now! Would you like to meet him?"

*****

It was that very same evening that Eleanor found herself waiting to be picked up by a driver; she was a little apprehensive but had no real misgivings being the personification of the description intrepid. At seven in the evening, the door buzzer sounded and Eleanor put on her red and blue anorak, picked up her shoulder bag and walked out of the door and towards the lift. The silver doors of the lift opened upon being summoned and within minutes, Eleanor was in a rather dilapidated bright green car with a strange man, being driven to a rendezvous that she did not know, and all because she had been and still was intrigued by the idea of meeting a Shaman. During the journey, Eleanor did become a little perturbed and due to the fact, that despite her attempts to strike up conversation with the driver he hardly responded and throughout the journey. Eleanor resolved that his lack of communication was probably due to the traffic being quite heavy at that time of night. It was when the car came to a halt that Eleanor got the surprise. The driver turned to look at her, smiled and spoke.

"We are here, Eleanor!"

Eleanor was sure that she hadn't given the man her name and this preoccupation caused her to worry a little right up until the driver pointed towards a red door on the front of a rather dilapidated building which was almost crowded out of sight by other people crammed on to the steep steps leading up to it.

"I'll wait for you here," the driver said.

"Oh, aren't you coming?" Eleanor asked of the driver not realising that she had raised her voice. The driver smiled.

"Don't worry. You are expected, Eleanor. I'll be waiting here," he said quietly as if trying to reassure her.

Eleanor turned and went towards the door and as she turned she noticed that all the people who were once crowding the thoroughfare had gone. Unperturbed, Eleanor strode boldly up to the door and gave a few loud raps with the black door knocker which seemed to be the only means by which she could gain the attention of anyone on the inside. Eleanor didn't have to wait long. The bright red door was opened immediately by an old and wizened faced woman, dressed in traditional Inuit clothes.

"You must be Eleanor, come in, the Shaman has been expecting you; he has just returned." she said bowing slightly to welcome her.

Eleanor followed the old Inuit woman into a room filled with people of all shapes and sizes, all of whom were wearing traditional Inuit dress. The sound of repetitive percussion veritably accosted her ears, and she noticed immediately that both rattles and drums were being used. Then she saw an old wrinkled faced man sitting cross legged at the back of the room; he wore what looked like a light decorated sealskin jacket and matching boots. The sounds abruptly stopped as the Shaman spoke.

"And so, I travelled searching beyond the land, the sea and the stars, then unto the land and the sea and the stars where the flower grows in the field and where the fish swims in the ocean and all is not well, for conflict war and destruction are on every horizon and all whilst the ice melts into the oceans, all whilst the poison of all life has days of promise."

He then raised both arms to the ceiling and started to recite.

Come ye the sun,
Come ye the photons of life,
Come ye the moon,
Come ye the tide in temptation,
Come ye the coral's sperm,
Go into the ocean's womb.

He then looked straight at Eleanor and spoke again.

"The teacher will find the pupil or the pupil will find the teacher; it just depends on who is measuring the stride of the other. I must travel again, and I will be gone for a long time, for the Gods demand my attention. I will take you with me, Eleanor!" he said looking straight at her eyes and continued briefly, **"From time to time!"** The Shaman then closed his eyes and all the percussion instruments began to sound again.

Eleanor was confused by the comments made and even more confused as the older and wizened face lady immediately led her back out towards the front door. Eleanor was back in the car that she had arrived in and within minutes, somewhat confused, she spoke to the driver immediately.

"He said that he would take me with him on his journey and from time to time! What did he mean?"

The driver turned to look straight at Eleanor and seemed to be smiling inwardly to himself as he regarded Eleanor's confused looking face.

"Do not worry! The Shaman is good!" and he then turned back to face the windscreen, started the engine and began to drive. On the way back to her flat, the driver, much to Eleanor's surprise, started to talk.

"It is a fact Eleanor that when mankind first arrived from the sea over two hundred thousand years ago, he was obliged to keep his family safe from harm, for he did not know the land as well as he did the oceans which had been his home since the Miocene. Our belief is that Orca first arrived on land as part wolf, and he roamed the earth until he became man. Then he organised security, for he knew of the predators who stalked the woods and forests of rain. Then he built defences to keep out the unwanted intruder whether they were man or beast, and then he built society which later developed into civilisations. Everything came in that order, Eleanor; safety, security, defence, society and last of all the civilisations and without this order neither society nor any civilisation would ever have existed and only anarchy would have prevailed. Now, today, nothing is safe again, for nothing is sacred anymore; the quest for too much power and the misconceptions of man has caused this to occur. These idioms have heralded the end of many civilisations in the past, and these idioms have yet again surfaced to start ages upon ages of competition and conquest which will jeopardise the stability of this civilisation; a civilisation by the way that had only just begun to accommodate a world of difference."

The car sped on through the evening traffic and towards Eleanor's apartment on Granville Island. The words which the man spoke seemed to her to have been delivered as if he were attempting to teach her something, although, she knew not what. There was silence for a while and Eleanor began to wonder what it was that the Shaman meant, *"I will take you with me,"* he had said and then *"From time to time!"* It was just at that point in the journey home, and as they were crossing Granville Bridge that the driver resumed talking.

"We are all of us on a journey, Eleanor, and yours is a special one! Fear nothing! If you believe in the transient spirit world, then pain is but an illusion"

The car then quite suddenly pulled up to her address, and the driver continued to stare out of the windscreen and seemingly unto a beyond which Eleanor could not see. He resumed talking.

"We are supposedly surrounded by wise men, Eleanor but if history is anything to go by then we have a lot to worry about! First it was the strongest that prevailed as leader and then it was the wisest, and for a time thereafter, it was the wise man that reached upwards and built the castles in the sky and the zeniths of power that neither man nor woman will ever comprehend! These castles in the sky that I speak of are the beliefs of man and should not manifest themselves in resolutions or status quos, which stifle or hinder the progression of life on this planet. Both the strong man and the wise man made themselves kings of the earth, but they in turn were soon challenged by the keepers of the castles in the sky who will continue to come and go. I ask you

Eleanor, how many religions have there been on earth in the time that man has lived on earth?" Eleanor did not answer.

"I can only wonder," Eleanor replied.

"Well, there have been many, and at times they conflict with each other, all of them. I tell you this much, Eleanor; the power of man that is invested in conflict has had its day if the earth is to survive as a home for us all. The utmost crisis is appearing; this may be the result unless we all begin to believe in the transient spirit. We should all believe in the transient spirit, Eleanor. All of the children of the Gods do." The driver looked at his watch and then announced: "Now you are home, and I must bid you a good night." The driver then held out his hand and Eleanor took it. He then got out of the car and opened the door. Eleanor whilst alighting from the car bade him farewell, trying not to look confused.

"Goodnight and thank you!"

Eleanor had had a long day and decided that the recording of the hummingbird would have to wait as she was decidedly ready for bed, but as she went to close the blinds she saw a huge, **'Blue-Black Raven'**, peering at her from a vantage point of the veranda's railing. As she went to close the blind, the Raven twisted its eyes away from her being and soared upward into the night sky.

*****

Port Hardy had some lovely walks, but the road down to the dockside wasn't particularly one of them. It wasn't that it was unkempt land rather it was wild and untamed, leaving one with the impression that the far horizons of oceanic domain lay beyond the jetty. The Professor had been waiting on board of the marine survey vessel, 'Ocean Lady', and was in the process of checking last minute details; he had been taking inventories of equipment and watching with the Captain as the equipment was checked. First, there were the new hydrophones to look over, and then there was the crane. The Professor was also waiting for the Canadian governments representative to arrive; he or she, whosoever it might be, were responsible for checking the safety of the barge that was to be towed out to the sound with the installations on board. Then there was all the diving equipment being used during deployment, and the remote-operated vehicle which was going to be used to tow the installations through the water, not to mention the installations themselves, one of which was constructed such that its form resembled a shoal of fish which would turn and twist in natural fashion as it moved through the water; this was to be the most important experiment of all. Finally, the Captain had to ensure that the hydrophone systems worked perfectly with the sonar equipment on board The Ocean Lady; they were state of the art and had the ability to record the high and low frequency communications of Orca. It was eight o'clock in the morning, and the Professor had decided to pick Eleanor up from her apartment to ensure that everyone was on station at the right time. The Professor was praying that the installations would arrive on time; by all accounts a pod of Orcas was on its way towards them and the installations had to be ready for the experiments. The Professor had had a lot of trouble arranging for the design and construction of the installations; they had been designed in the United Kingdom by two of the world's most renowned installation artists but each was fabricated in Canada. The Professor had decided that this was the best way to ensure integrity in respect of readiness and fitness for purpose. The whole operation was costing the Oceanic Institute a lot of money and the Professor was a little concerned about the budget, he wanted both the installations and the Orcas to arrive on time, but the

Mounted Police arrived before the truck had, and he had been interviewed. The Professor was told that the morning before, the truck which was holding the installations had been broken into, the driver had been murdered. It was a robbery but un-known to the Professor, photographs had been taken of each installation, which had been standing in blocks in the back of the truck. Everything including the lock had been put back in its place so as not to cause the suspicion that the installations had been tampered with.

Chapter 3
Simon

Simon leant on his oars exhausted, barely able to look across at the Cambridge boat but peering across one of the balanced oars he did see a man crying, sobbing, as if all the world was lost. Simon felt his shoulder slapped heavily by the man and boy seated right behind him, but in that state of exhaustion that knows no life, he was unable to turn; the pain in his legs and in his lungs was desperate to return to a normality which would enable him to smile and then to cheer. Another slap on the shoulder and this time he was able to turn and hug the crew member seated behind him but guilty feeling crept upon him and his mind wished his emblazoned blue eyes to wander across the line of his now flagging oar and towards the Cambridge boat, but the boat, an adversary in time, had gone.

*****

Simon was in the upper reading room of the Bodleian library at Oxford when he began to have his doubts. It wasn't the exhaustion that he had felt after competing in the boat race that provided that doubt; for he was back to his old self studying as hard as he could and even his hands were healing well. He took a good look at them, turning his hands in his lap so that he could see the worst of his wounds. It was his choice of career that was worrying Simon, for he knew very well that not being a wealthy student might have prejudiced his better thinking. However, he also knew that the salary offered had had to be important; debt was a constant angst for him. He had had an interview with SETI and he'd been offered a position. Simon was tired though and entirely because the regime of constant rowing together with the hours needed for academic study had caught up with him a little, still he was well aware that the witching hours would soon be upon him and he would be on the train down to Southampton to go to a party which he had been invited to and now that the race had been won. For the whole of the Oxford crew and the Cambridge crew for that matter, winning was everything and losing was an abyss from which one never returned. He had, before the race, dreaded the black thoughts and his mind wandered back to the rower in the Cambridge boat who had broken down on losing. His thoughts then ran back to his forthcoming career; Simon didn't really know whom to turn to for advice; of course, everyone seemed to be pleased that he was 'Going into Outer Space!' Such was the humour of his crewmates, but his reservations were creeping in day by day. The trouble was that his thesis concentrated almost entirely on the interpretation of sound in communications which was, to some just the science of phonetics, but to others his study was much more. It was true that SETI had projected good prospects for him but that was only if they found another WOW signal and the prospect of that happening given the time that they had been considering the constellations for extra- terrestrial signals, seemed now to be rather remote. As the days flew by since his interview, Simon increasingly saw himself sitting at a SETI desk in America with headphones on, twiddling his thumbs. Then there was the equation that they had showed him; the Drake Equation in fact, and the one that projected the possibility of finding other life in the Universe. He had looked at the premise for that equation and decided that for all intents and purposes the equation was merely a series of hypotheses built upon nothing more than other hypotheses. On top of this preoccupation of Simon's, there had been questions about the existence of 'Black Holes' in the magazine 'The Scientists Eye'. Evidently, an eminent Professor had suggested that black holes were nothing more than planets disappearing in the eyes of radio telescopes and as they sped away faster than speed of light. Simon was told by another student and he suggested that this was why these so called black holes were getting smaller and darker. At that juncture, whilst he was sitting in the Bodleian Library, the whole question of space discovery was in question. His mind wandered a little to a conversation that yet another student had had with him. Evidently the 'Black Hole' question opened the door on the mathematical relationship between quantum mechanics and Einstein's theory of relativity but Simon knew only too well that the subject of astrophysics wasn't the field of any of these students or indeed Simon's for that matter and he had withdrawn rather hurriedly from the conversations; in any event Simon later learned that this new theory had been dispelled by leading proponents in the field. Still, one thing was leading to another and speculative comments that had been made about the real and tangible knowledge gained by theorists in space exploration were not helping him to feel comfortable with his decisions to date. Simon was beginning to wonder how much they the scientists really knew in any field of endeavour, and at that point in time, whilst sat in the Bodleian library at Oxford, he wondered if he was on the right path. History, he mused, was strewn with misconceived discoveries but he also knew that the human race were bound to continue on a journey that yielded up truth, if only because hidden deep within the secret passages of mankind's DNA, was the instinct that made them explorers. Simon broke away from his preoccupations, looked at his watch, closed the text book open in front of him and got up from the desk. It was Friday. Tomorrow he would travel down to Southampton where he intended to have the time of his life.

*****

The late winter snow which was veritably billowing was beginning to blind both Simon and the friend that was accompanying him. There was no wind off the sea and all of this was extremely unusual for Southampton. As they approached their destination, it appeared to both of them that the apartment was a tad up market, at least from the outside. There was loud music coming from inside; at least he was sure that that the sound was coming from inside. Simon took the invitation from his coat pocket and pulled his collar up around his neck; the winter cold kept him shivering. The invitation read;

> To Simon Hamilton.
> Be there or be Square!
> Black Tie,
> 48 Hood Terrace, Ocean Village,
> Southampton.

"We're here, Simon!" Simon looked away from the preoccupation he had had of staring at his shoes whilst hiding his eyes from the unusual blizzard that had beset them both.

When his friend looked at him, he laughed.

"My my, my, you do look a mess; you've grown an icy beard!" his friend shouted.

Simons muffled retort came through the Oxford University scarf that they were both proudly wearing although, his friends face was exposed to the blizzard, to Simon it was as if his friend hadn't a care in the world.

"You absolutely love this weather, don't you? Tell me for God's sake, why!" Simon retorted.

"I'm from up North of course! You are a southern softy," his friend responded.

"Up North is all cold winds and chip butties and you are fatter than me which is why you don't feel the cold! Wait a minute! Have you been sunning yourself in the solarium again? Beware Gungadin, if Gwendoline finds out that would be tantamount to giving her permission to go to work with a Tiger Tank," Simon answered. Laughter ensued.

His friend put on a serious air, "I didn't know you'd studied history."

"Oh come on, let's find out if this is the right address!" Simon replied.

The snow had abated and both young men stood in awe before the front door and watched a **'Blue-Black Raven'** perched upon the fence that lay before the perimeter of the building. The **Raven** kept twisting its head from side to side watching them both before it twisted its head away and soared up into the early evening sky. Simon and his friend both watched the magnificent bird disappear. Without saying a word they both checked the address; the right number glistened in copper on the front door; he quickly pressed the doorbell, then again and again. Somebody turned the music up even louder prompting Simon to start banging loudly on the door. Quite suddenly the door opened and his eyes met with those of a vivacious young lady. The young lady was about his age and wore a close fitting pink bra and a very tight pair of hot pants; apart from a pair of pink high heel shoes and a tiara, she wore nothing else. Thinking that they had the wrong address Simon began to stutter.

"I...I am terribly sorry, we appear to have been given the wrong address. Is this where Eleanor lives?"

The girl started laughing and raised her hand to cover her mouth.

"Oh don't worry, Eleanor is in the kitchen with the other monkey suits. Come on in!"

Peter walked inside as the girl attempted to stifle her laughter.

"Can I take your coat your majesty; it is your majesty, isn't it? Oh, look you even have cufflinks!"

"Oh no, I'm not a member of the Royal Family; why are you expecting one of the Royals?" Simon stuttered still dismayed at the attire of the young lady standing before him.

"No but we have invited quite a few of the top brass!" the girl answered now laughing at the top of her voice and leading both Simon and his friend across the threshold of the front door and into the hallway.

Simon was not a little bemused followed the young lady into the kitchen and was immediately greeted with loud cheers by an assortment of young ladies wearing bikinis and high heels, and young men wearing nothing less than formal dress suits with bow ties although, some of the young men had discarded the dress jackets and wore the bow ties in dangling fashion. "Hoorahhhhhh!" one of the young men yelled and another shouted "Have a tipple!" Both young men suddenly became aware that virtually all the partygoers were drinking champagne.

"What is your tipple?" a voice shouted out.

"Well done on winning the boat race by the way; which of you is Simon, and which of you is David? I'm Mike, I've been invited along as a greeter, but take no notice if old Chubby over there refers to me as Greta, I call him Hansel, we think it's love!"

"Yes, the young man, named Chubby, piped up; he wants to marry me, but his dowry isn't big enough!" There was more laughter.

"Oh, I'm David, and this sorry excuse for an explorer is Simon; without me he'd never have got out of bed this morning." Simon's friend retorted whilst taking a bottle of champagne from the young lady who had greeted them both at the front door.

"Both out last night then?" another young lady's voice sounded from the back of the kitchen.

Simon had a bottle of champagne shoved into his hand and was watching the other party guests quickly followed the example set; nearly all of the guests, with the exception of the ladies, were drinking the champagne from the necks of the bottles; Simon felt at home immediately.

"We've arrived on the right planet then!"

"You most certainly have!" one of the girls shouted out from her repose on the corner of the drinks table. It was Eleanor.

Simon looked around and witnessed what he thought was an absolute vision. Eleanor was tall with long legs and a figure to die for; she had short, blonde hair which was slightly curled, but the eyes said it all; she was, he knew immediately, very intelligent. Simon was almost immediately slapped on the shoulder by another partygoer and conversation began on all manner of subjects, whilst laughter rang through the very vestibules of the kitchen and hallway and right up, until all were pleasantly inebriated. By three o'clock in the morning, all had moved from the kitchen to almost every room in the apartment. Celebrations were in full swing right up until the early hours when some guests started to leave, but the party had quietened down to a whisper at four thirty in the morning, with just a few of those that had been invited left in the apartment's open-plan sitting room. Simon was standing by the panoramic windows looking out at sea when he heard his friend David remonstrating with another guest.

"I disagree, that man's ideology is only prejudicing democracy by selling anarchy." His friend's head was bobbing and weaving from side to side as if he was watching a fly. "And with the view to organising alternative protocols," he said rather loudly, his emphatic nature being even more exposed by the amount of alcohol he had drunk.

"And once the battle for anarchy is won?" the other guest asked whilst being rather worse for having drunk far too much as well.

"Why; anarchy will be put to death by its main proponents, and all that will live thereafter will be the undemocratic oligarchs. Does communism spring to mind?" The conversation was hijacked by another guest.

"Oh, and one thing to remember; Hitler used the very same tactics before coming to power in the 1930s; Fascism and Communism, see if you can taste the difference. History couldn't!"

Then there was an outburst by a young woman who had had far too much to drink whilst the music centre played an old piece of classical music.

"Don't you see? You're all stupid, all of you, if you don't see it. It's not just the Russians; it's us as well. None of us trust each other. Communication is the problem and education! How do you expect a Russian peasant with no formal education to stop at the threshold of a war that their masters tell them is important if they want to save their motherland! How do you… Oh God! I don't want to go to war…"

The young lady then collapsed in a heap onto the carpet. Other partygoers ran to her aid, pulled her to her feet before sitting her down on a sofa. She was out for the count. Simon, slightly taken aback, and tired of the seriousness of political discourse, walked toward the stairwell that would take him to the toilet. It was, as he walked down the stairs that someone grabbed his arm.

"Simon! Have you heard the news? The Russians are threatening to invade Eastern Europe; we could all be called up!" Simon just looked at the other partygoer and continued towards the toilet.

"It's no laughing matter, Simon. It's true! We're all going to be called up!" the fading voice sounded as Simon disappeared along a short corridor.

Simon approached the door of the bathroom, knocked politely and then entered; only to find two other party-goers debating upon yet another subject. Simon recognised them both as members of the Cambridge boat crew. They were talking loudly.

"Japanese Imperialism was a major problem, and there is another, raising its ugly head right now. These people, if we should call them that, have no respect for life, and they have the genius to promise themselves more than can be attained by them on earth!" one said.

"Only the ignorant buy it, and as you are aware, armed with the confidence that the real strategist imbues in their rather stupid minds, namely money and weapons; then they become very dangerous indeed," The other replied.

Simon, remembering the young man whom he had seen crying after the race, joined in the conversation whilst urinating against the urinal receptacle and thinking that he could throw a little humour into the debate.

"It's all the fault of Viking mercenaries fighting for money during the Byzantium; they brought their tradition of dying with a sword in their hands and Valhalla with them, and some of their adversaries copied their beliefs!" but nobody was listening. Simon heard more of their conversation which again was tainted by the influence of too much alcohol.

"Hitler did the same, he used Röhm's Brownshirts, and then he had them all killed. That's the real prospect for those that fight for nihilism. The real strategists play the earthly game. The problem is, in the meantime, for us all!"

At that juncture, one of the Cambridge boat crew turned around to face Simon as he turned towards the door.

"It's Simon, isn't it; well done, old chap! We didn't come over to congratulate you I know, but you understand. Oh to hell with it! Anyway, we're both up for it next year, and we'll win! Did you hear about the Russians?"

Simon decided to leave the two partygoers and went back upstairs to the open plan living area where almost everyone that left had now congregated. It was as he reached the top of the stairs that the hostess, Eleanor, touched him on the arm. Simon turned to face her.

"And how are you, Simon? I was told to invite you. You've studied languages at Oxford, haven't you? And evidently you've studied computer science with mathematics!"

Simon turned to face Eleanor and was momentarily mesmerised.

"Well, not exactly. I have actually been studying the origins of language as well as mathematics and computer science. What's all this about the Russians?"

"Oh, they are just threatening war again, Simon. Look, don't worry; they do that every time they run out of Vodka!

Listen, what I want to know is this; what are you going to do now that you have finished studying?"

Simon had already warmed to Eleanor's sense of humour and was in the mood to talk. "Well, I am going to join SETI!" Simon replied.

"SETI? Isn't that the search for extra-terrestrial intelligence?" Eleanor asked.

"Yes, it is." Simon replied and quickly tried to engage Eleanor into a longer conversation.

"Oh, you have heard about SETI then."

Eleanor leaned back against the wall and regarded Simon closely.

"So, you are looking for another 'WOW' signal, but what I cannot understand is why all of that money and investment is being put in place searching for ET when we have a species right here on our planet which we cannot understand at all! Just think of what the Killer Whale could tell us about the oceans and probably much more!" Simon was all ears.

"Yes, take Orca for example; Orca has a sophisticated form of communication which we, at the Oceanographic Institute, are doing our best to interpret!" Eleanor took a sip from her champagne flute and watched him intently.

"Orca?" Simon enquired of Eleanor inquisitively.

"The Killer Whale! The whale has been around for about twelve million years or more, Simon. We, on the other hand, have only been here for two hundred thousand years or more. Look, I'll cut to the mustard, as you boys say. We were given an indication of your thesis by Oxford, and we want you to consider joining us at the Oceanic Institute. Would you like a tour?"

It occurred to Simon that he had just heard another 'wow' signal.

Chapter 4
The Professor

Waterloo station buzzed with life as Simon and his friend sat eating the breakfast that they had both bought from one of the fast food stalls. People of all walks milled about, some looking upwards toward the boards which announced arrivals destinations and departure times; the platforms were indicating as and when the trains were ready for boarding. Simon kept his eye on the board directly in front and above his vantage point of chairs that had been installed for waiting passengers. A pigeon flew close to Simon, and he quickly lifted his leg forward to scare it away, but it only moved a few yards and then started to wander in its own fashion, its body waddling from side to side back towards them looking for the odd crumb that might have dropped from bread rolls, and if they were lucky from the fillings themselves. A young girl, wearing a bright yellow coat, was busy taking photographs, and whilst standing in one of the queues a lady, who appeared to be her mother, began panicking after yet another dirty grey pigeon had flown just above her head. Simon had not taken his eye off **'The Raven'** that he had seen peering down at him from the rafters but was jolted into movement by an announcement that his train, the one to Southampton, was ready for boarding.

"Come on, Gunga Din, that's us!" he said as he turned to face his friend and colleague who was still munching away at his breakfast bap.

"I'm ready!" his friend returned.

"Well, let's get a move on; we haven't got allocated seats, and we need to make sure we get seated; don't forget that it's still a bank holiday for lots of people."

"You wouldn't think so what with the weather and all," his friend complained and continued as they moved with their overnight bags towards their platform.

"What I don't understand is what blinding blizzards and cold weather have to do with global warming and in April of all times of year; it's supposed to be Spring isn't it?"

"I have it on good authority that Spring does not start until next year," Simon yelled behind him as he hurried forward towards the barrier and in front of his friend who was still munching away on his breakfast bap whilst walking alongside the carriages in a very nonchalant manner.

Within what must have been minutes both Simon and his friend were embarking on to a carriage, already crammed full of people some of whom were already placing their bags in overhead racks. Simon found two seats on the right that were facing each other and that hadn't been taken. They were by a window which would give them both a view of the passing terrain as they travelled; there were no tickets that claimed places for other travellers. Simon duly sat down whilst handing his overnight bag and overcoat to his friend, who was having a terrible time avoiding people traffic still arriving to look for vacant seats. At ten minutes past the hour, a whistle sounded outside and the train's engines started to reverberate; the train slowly pulled away from Waterloo station on a cold, grey and seemingly wintery Monday morning.

"Typical, I do all the hard work," his friend announced to Simon, still clasping the half-eaten breakfast bap in his hand as he sat down.

Both looked out of the window at a London they were leaving behind for interviews that they were barely interested in; his friend having arranged to visit a company in Southampton that specialising in a subject which Simon knew nothing about whatsoever. Whilst looking out of the window, Simon began to think about Eleanor, the Marine Biologist, who had thrown the party. Eleanor had arranged for him to meet with the Professor of the Oceanic Institute and he wasn't too sure that his scepticism wouldn't get the better of him. Still he was going back to Southampton yet again but before he could think of anything else his eyes closed and fell into a deep sleep. He arrived at the Oceanographic Institute on time.

*****

"Well, this might seem a different place to start!" the Professor said looking closely at Simon as if he was inspecting him, "I'm going to ask you a question. Are you a Christian?"

"Well, yes I am Professor," Simon responded, "I have been known to bless myself now and again," Simon started laughing thinking that more absurd questions were to follow.

"When was that, Simon?" the Professor asked rather seriously.

"Oh, that was after we'd won the boat race," Simon replied rather whimsically now wearing a soberer demeanour.

The Professor then smiled briefly whilst taking an even longer and more serious look at Simon and then resumed.

"Well I too, just like you were born a Christian, but I have my reservations. Do you?"

"Well, I can only speak for myself, but well, yes of course I do, Professor; being a Scientist I have trouble with various concepts. I believe in Jesus Christ and God but that's as far as I go."

The Professor resumed talking.

"Listen Simon, the only reservations I have comes alive when I count the beliefs that man has had in the time we have had on this earth and then I wonder which one is the correct one and whether any one of us will ever have the insight to determine the will of God. And yet there is not one of us that live on this earth that does not reach up towards the heavens in order to capture the word of God and the peace that we all strive for. I have come to reconcile that Christianity provided for two thousand years or more of stability at a time when the average man and woman lived between the idioms of power and fear, education was and still is the key to comprehension but I take exception when articles such as this front-page news tell me that I shouldn't continue in my quest."

The Professor then reached into his draw and showed Simon an article which he had cut out from a periodical.

"What's this?" Simon asked and began to read. "Oh, I see, God made man in his own likeness and did not give the Earth another intelligent species!"

Simon handed the article back to the Professor.

"Let's move on a bit. By all accounts, Jesus Christ was an extremely intelligent person who by his own admission was a host for higher intelligence which his miracles bore testimony to. For those of us who say that finding God is enough I say this 'God is the Lord of all creation' and we are supposed to find God every day, and that includes placing an emphasis on scientific research, no matter what the Christian right think or any other denomination for that matter. I doubt very much that God would frown upon our search for the scientific reality, or perhaps I should say realities, for the science we are looking for does not come from within ourselves, it is already here. We are and have only ever been in the process of discovering God in science with only our developed technology which is as yet, I'm afraid to say, still in its infancy."

"What is it that you are trying to say, Professor?" Simon asked.

"You are a first-class student in philology and linguistics and you understand computational mathematics. I understand from Eleanor that you wrote a thesis titled 'Translating the Language of the Unknown Species', I would be very interested in reading your work but you have to be aware that there are many people who will not like our investigations."

"Well, I am not worried about the critics, I will oblige Professor," Simon replied.

The Professor continued.

"Now we come to the crux of the matter. What concerns me is this; you want to join SETI and search the stars for another intelligent species which scientists say may not look or think anything like the human race, then the task would be to translate their language such that we could communicate with them. Well, all evidence suggests that despite that ET in all probability is out there, the distances involved are quite obviously detrimental to our ability to either communicate directly or to translate. In any event the likelihood of anyone finding another WOW signal such as was discovered on that narrowband radio signal received by the 'Big Ear' radio-telescope at the Ohio State University way back in 1977 is pretty remote, don't you think? I know it's interesting, the SETI project and I do not wish to prejudice your thinking but I would like to entice you towards our programme. I say that everything that you're looking for is right here on Earth."

The Professor then busied himself setting up a projector which took up position at the back of the room.

"I now come to Orca. Just imagine what could happen if we could translate the language of the Killer Whale! The people of the earth that we live on would then really be transformed by the realisation that we are not the only intelligent species on this planet or in the 'Universe', and going back to my initial question on God I doubt very much that the men of God and of whatever denomination would be annoyed at our quest for scientific understanding once they realise the benefits of such translation. I am not saying that the scientists will reveal more than what is already written but man has always been on a quest for new beliefs and beginnings. Translating Orca's language would in fact suffice to install a necessary improvement in human relations by eliminating misconceptions and bring to focus the necessity to take real care of the environment on Earth" Simon listened whilst the Professor continued.

"The stakes are high I'm afraid. The Earth is in danger of ecological collapse and we are, right here in the United Kingdom, looking for solutions and more so than any other 'Nation State on Earth'. We have always been leaders in scientific enquiry and we will continue to be so. Of course, it is entirely your decision whether you join us or not but my seminar this morning is designed to entice you to do just that. Going back to SETI briefly, the Oceanographic Institute would like to approach SETI and ask them if we could use their worldwide computing facilities to translate the language but alas I fear they have other plans for the computing capacity that they have. We have now, and as SETI did, appealed to the British public and set up a network that harnesses computing power across these islands of ours and in much the same way that they have, but there is scope for improvement and that means getting other countries involved."

The Professor smiled as he pulled down a screen at the far end of the room. He then pulled a seat up for Simon to sit upon but before he could pull all of the blinds over the windows to a close, both Simon and he became aware that they were being watched. An enormous **'Blue Black Raven'** was perched on one of the window sills. They both stood as if mesmerised by the bird as it twisted its neck from side to side whilst peering at them and before it quite suddenly opened its wings and flew into the sky beyond. The Professor pulled the shutter down and resumed talking.

"The Institute has just completed a forty-year study of the Killer Whales, Orcinus orca's communication systems, and we are now moving into a new phase of our investigation. We have found that Orca has a sophisticated method of communication that is both uniform and complex. Orca's sonar is far in advance of human capability because it is, for want of a better description, gyroscopic in transmission and reception capability and we at the institute believe that Orca also reads from its sonar emissions, which means that they pick up any occurrence or objects of interest in the water." The Professor then switched a projector on and pointed at the screen. "Take a look at this; it's a spectrograph reading of samples taken of Orca's high and low frequency transmissions within Puget Sound in Canada and over that forty-year period I was just talking about. This film shows new installations being placed and towed in Puget Sound. We wanted to test Orca's intelligence a little further than it had been prior to this year. We have found that the Killer Whales multidimensional reception capability is both complex but most of all it is multichannel. It is a necessity for everyone to realise and appreciate that Orca's communicative ability is not frustrated by other acoustic disturbances in the hydrosphere. I've relayed this fact to all of the team who are ecstatic, we are now certain that we are on the right track."

The Professor then stood back and allowed Simon to watch the ten-minute documentary. Simon was glued to the screen taking in the pictures of huge dorsal fins of an Orca pod as they swam in concert alongside the Oceanographic Institutes seagoing vessel 'Ocean Lady' and the submerged installations that the Professor had been talking about. When the film had finished, the Professor turned on the lights in the room and switched off the projector.

"I want to show you a sample of the results from our study, Simon", and then he switched the projector on again, the lights were turned off again and the Professor continued to speak. "These particular readings are specific to the designed installations being placed in the water this year. The study included differently designed installations for alternate shoals of fish and other objects."

The screen showed graphical representations of Orca's language on a spectrograph which was a special piece of recording equipment. The spectrograph readings jumped across the screen until the Professor froze the pictures. He had a small rod in his hand with which he used to point.

"You see this jump in the readings between A and B which are marked here and here, well they are commensurate with readings which we had taken from Orca whilst he or she was reading in sound. Orca was reading our installations; we know this because there are no repeats in any of the readings we have taken in over forty years of study!"

Simon sat back and regarded the spectrograph and then got up and walked to the side of the screen.

"Do you mean to tell me that the Orca can read in sound, Professor?" Simon asked showing a first sign of astonishment.

"That, Simon, is fact!" the Professor replied.

*****

Early in April, Simon found himself being given a tour by Eleanor, a Canadian photographer named Peter and the Professor at the Oceanographic Institute. He walked alongside the Professor as the Professor pointed out the facilities that harboured the departments of Marine Biology, Oceanography, Marine Geochemistry, and Marine geosciences.

"I have been here nearly ten years, and in that time we have made great strides Simon. Today we are fully equipped with a state of the art marine survey vessel 'Ocean Lady' which travels all over the world. We are currently preparing to make a trip to the Barents Sea. I shall be going along with Eleanor and eight of our other scientists, if you jump into the car with me we'll drive down to the dock and I'll take you on board for a look."

Eleanor looked towards Simon. Simon smiled broadly at her. "That would be great, Professor."

It took precisely ten minutes for the Professor to drive to the gates of the dock and before Simon knew what was happening he was standing in front of a blue coloured hull with red and white coloured topsides. The Ocean Lady was at least eighty feet long.

"Come on Simon, let's climb aboard," Eleanor shouted.

Simon followed Eleanor and the Professor up the gangplank and along the deck towards the bridge. The steep stairwell was painted in gleaming white. The three of them pulled hard on the white railings whilst moving upwards towards the door of the bridge. The Professor opened the door and waited for Eleanor and Simon to go inside. They were greeted by the Skipper.

"Hello Eleanor, good morning, Professor, we will be ready for sea on time, I'm just loading the last of the provisions."

"This is Sven Vynchenko, my navigating officer and this is Angus, our captain; Angus is a true Scot and according to Sven, Angus is the foreigner on board, aren't you Angus? Sven is Ukrainian," the Professor said.

"Good morning all," the navigating officer returned whilst laughing with Angus and then continued, "Do not forget Sven that you are also a foreigner!" Then everyone laughed. Sven then turned his attention to the chart table.

"What about the new sonar equipment; has it all been installed and commissioned?" the Professor asked.

"Yes, it was all tested at sea; everything is functioning as it should; it is fantastic you know," Angus answered whilst smiling at Eleanor. He continued talking.

"The Professor and his team helped develop the new sonar equipment; we call it SEDNA."

"Why SEDNA?" Simon asked.

"Oh, it is the name the Inuit give to the goddess of the sea!" Eleanor replied and then she introduced Simon. "This is Simon, our latest recruit, he'll be analysing the data on the spectrogram for us."

"Welcome aboard Simon," Angus, the skipper, greeted.

Simon looked around at the array of equipment on the bridge and was astounded.

"How do you operate all of this equipment?" Simon asked.

"Well we have a full complement on the bridge at all times, a different watch for different times, day and night. I say day and night but by the time we reach the Arctic, the sun never sets; we'll be there during the summer solstice."

"Are you coming too Simon?" Angus asked.

"Well are you Simon?" Eleanor grabbed him by the arm and poked him in the ribs which almost hurt. She started to laugh that infectious laugh again.

The Professor looked Simon up and down with a fixed gaze.

"What are your sea legs like, my boy?"

"Oh, they are definitely good, Professor; I'd love to come with you; can I come with you?"

"Right, we'll get you kitted out for the trip; we will not be leaving for a month or so, but it will be at six o'clock in the morning; you'll be on board at five."

The Professor and Angus noticed that Eleanor's smile veritably lit up the bridge.

Eleanor went to sleep at eleven thirty that evening, she had had a long day and was grateful to be able to rest her head on her floral-patterned pillows that punctuated the top of her bed and on this particular evening it wasn't long before she fell into a deep and meaningful sleep full of adventure and full of fear.

*****

A field of corn swayed gently in the breeze whilst touching lightly the air above as if tempting the tips of golden ears to paint aloft with soft gentle strokes. Far above, a black and white seagull floated on sail like wings as if watching all that prevailed and just below wispy grey and white clouds that moved silently across the light blue sky. Beneath the field of corn, a small, grey adder made its way beneath a steel like cobweb that had strung itself between two stalks of corn, its web shining and glittering with drops of morning dew hanging like all of nature's jewels and all on show for the unsuspecting greenfly which flapped tiny wings ready for a last flight. A red and black spotted ladybird watched from a short distance and the sound of a cricket ground out a clicking tempo that lasted briefly. At the edge of the field, a tall, red and black poppy stood stiff and sentinel like alongside a yellow and white daffodil which in turn reached for the sky on a long green stalk; they were waiting for the sound to get nearer, waiting to be pollinated. Buzzzzzz, came the sound but both the stiff expectant, red and black poppy and the swaying yellow and white daffodil waited and waited.

Eleanor had been sleeping but something greatly disturbed her whilst asleep, it was as if she was being thrown from side to side and up and down in haphazard fashion. She was beginning to feel sick when she opened her eyes and only to be surprised by a panoramic view of a light blue sky with wispy cirrus clouds above her all of which seemed to be moving all over her field of vision, a seabird moved from side to side and up and down within her sight. Eleanor was flying way below the seabird but she couldn't navigate properly. Eleanor's instincts told her that she should not make for the two flowers that she could see at the far end of a field of corn that she was approaching but whatever was ailing her was prohibiting her navigational skills. She was making a loud sound as she flew in haphazard fashion Buzzzzzzzzzzz and like a pair of scissors she veritably cut a jagged path above the green and lush field below her and until she passed by a field of corn which was now beneath her. Eleanor knew that she had a task to fulfil but it wasn't to pollinate flowers. Unbeknown to Eleanor, her solar clock which told her how far she had flown from the hive had been affected by a pathogen, a disease was upon her, and she found difficulty in oscillating her wings which beat frantically against the cool afternoon airs. More than once she almost plummeted toward the ground but somehow, she managed to stay aloft. Eleanor was trying to make her way beyond her current field of vision and past two flowers at the end of the field of corn; the flowers, a poppy and a daffodil came into the sight of her panoramic vision and she flew straight past towards a hedgerow which she almost collided with. She then caught sight of **'The Raven'** who was watching her intently, then, before more than two or three seconds had passed, she crashed through man-made curtains that billowed slightly and which hung just beyond a French window. Eleanor was now upside down on a wooden floor and could hear voices getting louder and louder, a man's footsteps were approaching; she heard his voice.

"Damned bees everywhere, what's the matter with them all; they are all falling out of the sky." Footsteps were getting closer and closer. Eleanor tensed her very being for what was to come but another younger voice sounded.

"Don't father, don't tread on it! My teacher tells me that nearly half of the world's food supply depends on the bees, don't tread on it!" a younger voice rang out and within seconds Eleanor felt herself being carried in a white handkerchief towards a window sill in another room. Colourful walls with distinctive patterns and ornate ceilings passed her by before she was set down.

"There, I'll leave it just here until it gets better," the young boy's voice sounded out.

"You'd better come out of there. I've got an important meeting this afternoon. Go outside and play!" the man's voice responded.

Eleanor, now resting on the white window sill waited silently as vibro-acoustic sound, which she was able to interpret, reverberated through her body.

Chapter 5
Annabelle

A blue flag with a yellow diagonal cross flew in a quiet wind above the town hall. It was Wednesday, a market day in St Albans. All manner of people milled about and walked slowly up and down the market stalls eyeing the normal and then again what some might call the exotic. Couples and others walked past a picture-framing stall, then a stall which sold jewellery, another selling clothing, yet another selling all types of fruits, there was a stall that sold soft feta cheese and black and green olives alongside bright red sun-drenched tomatoes. All of the stalls were covered by blue and yellow canopies which shielded the fare from the rain; rain that was falling incessantly, yet not one of those just browsing or buying was disappointed. There was acoustic guitar music, a folk singer sat on a stall in a cobbled thoroughfare that led down to an old pub, he was singing 'Blowing in the wind'. Inside the pub called 'The Boot', good English bitter, together with lagers and ciders, were being served.

An older gentleman and a woman both with grey hair stopped briefly before a stall which sold army surplus. They walked slowly on and down an avenue in the direction which led to an entrance of St Albans Cathedral. There was a school in nearby grounds; their son had been a pupil there, but the man suddenly stopped and pulled at his wife, not wishing to pass near gravestones which lined a small commemorative garden.

"Come this way, I want to view the Cathedral from the park. We'll go through the arch shall we? We can take tea or a drink at the 'Fighting Cocks', then watch the swans and ducks."

Suddenly the Cathedral Bells rang, 'Dong, Dong, Dong, Dong, Dong, Dong, Dong, Dong, Dong, Dong!' The man looked at his watch and then his wife's face; she was looking at the cobbled ground and frowning again. It was 'Ten o'clock.' The man then whispered quietly in his wife's ear.

"Don't worry! Terry will be standing shoulder to shoulder with the finest and best mates in the world."

At that precise moment, but in a different time zone, their son and other British citizens were fighting for their lives. Russia had just invaded a country that was a member of NATO.

*****

And at this hour, a tall, confident man sat down at his desk and switched on the computer console. The console opened up to show a screensaver, depicting a picture of his home in Oxfordshire. He began to look at the picture of the detached house set as it was behind young, silver birch which loomed in front of what the man considered to be a perfect scene. Rustic leaves burnt by the sun brushed the small but tidy lawn's fading green grass; the assortment of different coloured flower beds briefly captured his imagination; birds had been singing on that day; he'd heard a song thrush sing. He lingered before the screensaver a little longer than he had done for a long time. In the picture, his wife and children were sitting at a small table which was situated at the rear of the house and in front of French styled windows; they were all smiling, and he knew that the smiles weren't for the camera, they were for him. *That's what cameras are really for!* he told himself, and then he arose from the desk, took off his blue suit jacket and hung it on the back of his chair. Suddenly, there was a knock at the door of his office, "Come in!" he shouted, his voice wearing a slight 'West Country' accent.

It was one of his directors. "Good morning, Sir, I've just brought you the file that you had asked for."

"Thank you, leave it on the table, I'll get to it in due course. Did you call the Home Office for me?"

"Yes, I did, Sir; as yet, they have not spoken to the Prime Minister." His director closed the door behind him.

This tall, dark haired gentleman who wore a constant wistful smile then turned his attention back to the computer sitting on his desk. He opened up his e-mail, and before he had read anything, he started to draft a communiqué.

From: The Director General,
To: Department 616-language translators.
Subject: Vigilance

With the advent of Russian aggression in Europe and Russian insurgency activities in the United Kingdom, I thought it prudent that I address all officers in the 'Translation Section'.

MI5 must be vigilant! The geopolitical landscape has changed with the threat of 'thermonuclear war'. As you are aware, Russia has invaded the territories of other nation states and is threatening other territories including the United Kingdom. You will not have missed the fact that tensions have also mounted within the EEC, with some states declaring themselves communist on the back of political upheaval. The Middle East is still in turmoil with the prospect of another conflict looming between Sunni and Shiite Moslems. Language translation and interpretation therefore, central to MI5's investigative work, is crucial.

As you are aware, there have been terrorist atrocities committed on mainland Britain in the past and public outcry has enticed Parliament to act. Since, the government has passed the telecommunications bill; it is now MI5's responsibility to listen to all forms of communication; the government deciding that it would not have been prudent to wait for a declaration of war before MI5 acted. Today, both MI5 and GCHQ, having completed specific programmes of development, to control highly sophisticated and networked computers which can sift the speech data strings of millions of mobile telephones and landlines. These sophisticated filters and sieves have the ability to isolate conversations which are associated with terrorism, espionage and insurgency and a significant number of the communications that we are interested in are coded. A target could in point of fact change his or her mobile phone many times but once they have been identified, the mobile or telephone number ceases to be the premise for investigation and the 'Decibel Signature' of the conversation is referenced. These 'Tracked Voices' which are registered in our 'Acoustic library;' have their very own acoustic signature. Once the voice is identified, the search is suffixed in binary code and references drawn from our databases which have the ability to log every call made or received in the United Kingdom. You might be looking for the proverbial 'Needle in a haystack' but always remember this; it is your job to find the needle!

One of the translators employed by MI5 was sitting at his desk at Thames House in London. The young man who came from an ordinary British family had been with the 'Secret Service' for six years now. He loved his job and never felt frustrated about the secrecy involved. At the beginning of his career, he had to mentally subtract from the convivial in front of friends so as not to reveal the true nature of his work, now however, such diversionary tactics were second nature. This morning, the young man was analysing a data string of communication. He could, if necessary call up other data strings on to his screen, all from the same family of acoustic signature, but he decided to go over this one again. The computer program had signalled that the speaker was Romanian. The particular piece of communication that he was listening to rang an alarm bell; it was out of context.

"The Killer Whales multidimensional reception capability is both complex but most of all it is multichannel. It is a necessity for hierarchies to appreciate, that its communicative ability is not frustrated by other acoustic disturbances in the hydrosphere."

The young man realised that the message was not coherent and pressed one of the F keys on the board in front of him. Within seconds the latest 'Enigma' machine was informing him of that the message was a virtual copy of a communication relayed by internet from the United Kingdom's Oceanographic Institute. He frowned and spoke aloud to himself.

"Whales? Why would Romanians want to follow what is happening at the Oceanographic Institute?"

The partially decoded transcript was then sent immediately by e-mail to his designated Intelligence Officer.

*****

At 10 am in the morning, a young woman in her early twenties walked her dog; a King Charles spaniel; a brown and white Blenheim along a path in the local wood. The young lady had stopped momentarily as she noticed an unusual bird which seemed to be watching her from the vantage point of a silver birch that had been not ten feet away from her, it was a **Raven**; she stood stock still so as not to disturb the bird which kept turning and twisting its head from side to side, never taking its eyes off of her. The young lady pulled the lead on her Blenheim close to her side as it began to bark at the **Raven** but it was to no avail, the **Raven** opened its wings and flew to a higher repose. The young lady resumed her walk musing that it had been a strange sight for she had seen much wildlife in the wood but had never spotted a Raven in that vicinity before. The young lady then met an elder lady with whom she had become acquainted on the path that was bordered by lush green ferns. "Good morning," the elder lady greeted. The elder lady quickly gathered her lead towards her side and calmed her Alsatian with a pat on its side.

"Good Morning, how is Fido today?" The old lady smiled knowing full well that the dog's title gave away a good sense of humour.

"Oh, he is much better Angela; he's back on his food again, it was my arm last night!"

The elder lady laughed until they both drifted into the convivial before each going on their respective ways. It was raining lightly and the leaves on the trees sounded the music like pitter-patter that the young lady simply adored. The rain reminded her of a little nugget that she had been given. *"Watch those little raindrops closely and one day they will paint the sky."* The Director General had given her the nugget on the first day that she joined the organisation. On leaving the wood, she looked back and only to see the Raven perched on a branch at the woods periphery.

Just like her colleagues, she had been born to an ordinary working family. Her father, who was from Tunbridge, was still a car mechanic and her mother, who had been born in Trinidad, again from a traditional family, worked a till in a local supermarket. Annabelle's younger brother was studying at the Royal College of Music, training to be the next revelation to hit the West End musicals. She had been studying 'European History' at a new but up and coming university when her imagination was stimulated by an advertisement for the Secret Service. Her parents were not surprised when she had told them that she had applied to join MI5; a bright and inquisitive student, she had all of the attributes necessary.

At twelve o'clock that morning, the same young person, a young lady of twenty-four years of age, was at her desk in Thames House and noticed that she had two new e-mails; she read them immediately, such was the ethos. The first email was from the Director General written earlier in the day, the second from one of the translators. Annabelle read both and then read the transcript which accompanied the second e-mail. Noticing the reference to sequence, she read the message again. The conversation it seemed was between a Romanian and a British national. Annabelle knew that she would need more information if she were to decipher the true meaning in the message.

*****

On a Saturday morning, a Romanian restaurant situated right in the middle of Tower Hamlets was raided by the 'Home Offices Immigration Police'. By lunchtime the very same day, Annabelle was sitting in a police cell listening to a man who called himself a refugee, procrastinating in broken English. The man looked like he hadn't washed for days and was dishevelled in appearance.

"I cannot find papers, I have passport but it's lost!"

Annabelle interrupted politely.

"May I have a word with him in private officer? I will call you when I've finished."

The cell door shut behind the police officer. Annabelle reached into her coat pocket and tossed the man a packet of cigarettes and a lighter; they were both Russian.

"Where did you get those?" Annabelle asked.

The man looked at the box of cigarettes and replied.

"Thank you, but I do not smoke."

"Your English is getting better, Dmitri; that's your real name, is it?"

"Let's talk about the conversation you had with a British national, Mr Ronan McGregor, who works in Scotland, at the Faslane Nuclear Submarine base, shall we?"

Annabelle pulled a black and silver coloured recorder out of her bag, placed it on the table and began to play the message. She then sat back in her chair and watched the man's reactions.

"That is not me!"

"Well if it is not you we'll just send you back to Romania, but we will let the Russians know that you were interrogated."

The lines of fear on the suspects face were quite evident.

*****

Ronan McGregor was sitting in a political rally in Glasgow when he was tapped on the shoulder by a plain clothes police officer.

"Can I talk to you for a minute or two, Ronan?"

Sometime later on that morning, Mr Ronan McGregor was sitting handcuffed in another police cell, three hundred miles from the previous interrogation that Annabelle had conducted. Annabelle, however, was now in Glasgow and at the police station, having caught a shuttle flight from Heathrow just three hours earlier. Just like the other prisoner, Mr Ronan McGregor had been told that he was being kept under 'The Prevention of Terrorism Act'.

Annabelle asked the suspect a question.

"Have you ever thought of what would happen to 'Bonnie Scotland' if the Russians invaded, or indeed if they ever got hold of secret information on British nuclear submarines, Ronan?"

Mr Ronan Michael McGregor looked frightened.

"It could well have been the same thing that would have happened to all of these islands of ours if it weren't for the RAF. You remember the words of Winston Spencer Churchill, don't you? Never in the field of human conflict…"

Before Annabelle could continue, Mr Ronan McGregor started to cry. Annabelle waited a few minutes for him to recover his faculties.

"Well…"

"I'll tell you everything. What is it that you want to know?" he stuttered.

*****

The very next day, Annabelle was back at her desk in Thames House; she was working on other business, but something was nagging at her; it was the conversation about the Whales. Yes, they had found out about the disclosure, but why the message? Annabelle was convinced there was more. A second interview with her suspect revealed nothing. The question, however, stayed with her, and she sent an e-mail to her line manager requesting his assistance. Annabelle's work and that of the translator's, which had been of paramount importance for it, was on that very day that the director general of MI5 told the Ministry of Defence that the specification for the 'Acoustic Protection' which entirely covered 'Britain's nuclear submarines' had been passed on to the Russians. At seven o'clock in the evening, Annabelle received an e-mail telling her that she was to liaise with a Lieutenant Commander Carmichael at the Oceanographic Institute in Southampton as soon as possible.

Chapter 6
The Cabinet

The Prime Minister, whilst sitting at the head of a burnt oak conference table began to address all members of the cabinet who peered at him above the glasses and bottles of mineral water that littered the damask linen. He stood up and looked all around him, and just beyond the environs of the table saw a **'Blue Black Raven'** perched upon the sill of one of the casement windows. The Prime Minister dispensed with his pipe which he was apt to carry with him at all times, and walked toward the window watching the bird as it was in turn watching him by crooking its neck from side to side. He stood for a moment in front of the bird that did not even flinch until he pulled up the casement window to let air in; only then did the **Raven** opened its wings and fly up into the afternoon sky. For some reason, he seemed to lose concentration, but he quickly gathered his thoughts and began to speak as he walked back to his seat at the head of the table.

"War is imminent, and the Russians have given the government of the United Kingdom an ultimatum, but let us not start with recriminations." He said holding his hand up to stop any interruption. "We, in the United Kingdom, will be the last ones to hold out even though we are seemingly on the back foot; I want to know everything, so please get the Lord of the Admiralty on the telephone as soon as this meeting has finished." As he spoke, he looked towards the assistant who was busy taking notes. The Foreign Secretary spoke up first.

"These problems have arisen because the Russians, having developed nuclear weapons, decided to provide these weapons to other nation states with similar politics, and in order to drive a wedge between the existing relationships that we in the United Kingdom had with our allies. It is no use blaming others for we in the West allowed it to happen by conceding too much of our philosophy to the realms of wishful thinking. We must always remember for the future that every political ethos is practical; this description 'political ethos' includes Communism, but I for one would not disagree when it is said that Communism is hardly ideal, and I know that I am not alone in this thinking. We must, all of us at this table today, remember that every political embargo enacted against us whether it is by proxy or by direct means is a threat to our way of life. The Russians sole purpose was to acquire ideological affinity by economic gain, and then power. Be sure of this! If there be, but one all-powerful Oligarch; it is him and we and the rest of the world are in danger. It was on our shoulders to wrestle the cap of power from his head. That is no longer the case, for if we dare we will lose! That is my assertion."

The Prime Minister then began to walk towards the sash windows once again; he looked down upon the honeybee that lay prostrate upon the sill and was about to sweep it onto the floor, but just as suddenly turned back towards those members of the cabinet that had attempted to keep his gaze.

"I'm expecting a call from none other than the Russian President during this next hour. I am expecting assurances from the President given the negotiations that have taken place. After all, we do have everything to lose, do we not? Let me put you under no illusions whatsoever; we live in very dangerous times. For any of you that are living under the illusion that power has its zeniths in government and Gods; be aware, the ultimate deterrent is brandished by some as the zenith to their cause, and we can no longer counter, we just do not have the resources!"

Another cabinet member spoke up. "But Prime Minister, our deterrent of nuclear weapons is and has always been here to counter the beyond of politics and diplomacy, and in case if either Communists or Oligarchs might like to brandish their weapons of mass destruction as the ultimate talking point; I for one doubt very much that they will use them. Let us not forget that our nuclear deterrent, and dare I say it theirs, is the cause of the peaceful coexistence that we have enjoyed up until today."

"And I fear to say that the Russian nuclear capability is, as I have said formidable and the very zenith of their political philosophy," The Prime Minister answered.

The Home Secretary spoke, "I believe that man will resolve his issues with one another; despots and oligarchs may come and go, and this one will go, mark my words; all we have to do is to remind him of his soft underbelly." The Home Secretary then stopped speaking and reached for a glass of water sitting on the table in front of him.

"A soft underbelly you say? And what might that be, Stephen?" The Prime Minister spoke to the Home Secretary directly. "You are right of course," then he held his hand up to stop any incursion into his thoughts. "Democracy; a very human desire, was born of the first ever dispute that ever caused pain. Fear of dying, fear of death amongst educated and civilised people is the same as love for life and having respect for life is the same as being on the road to Utopia. It might be too late in the day to sell these Communists a fear of death and paradoxically a love for life but by God we are going to give them pain that they understand so that they too will covet life! They will change, mark my words! We will not surrender our democracy quietly, and we will not make the same mistake twice!"

The Home Secretary then arose from his chair and carried a sheet of paper with him. "Prime Minister, here is the intelligence report reissued by the Home Office. The Russians have stolen the specification of the acoustic protection that covers the hulls of the UK's nuclear submarine fleet. The Russians have since informed the government of the United Kingdom that the whereabouts of all of our boats are known, and that they have been targeted. The Admiralty have given an order to all crews which effectively remove all of the boats from operations until a solution can be found. This leaves our nuclear deterrent completely nullified."

The Prime Minister glanced over the document and then asked a question.

"Have the Nuclear Non-Proliferation protocols gone that far?"

"I am afraid that they have," the Home Secretary replied and he continued.

"The United Kingdom, like so many other powers with nuclear deterrents, had negotiated with all of the superpowers. Those that sat on the Executive Powers Committee at the United Nations relinquished their nuclear arsenals at the beginning of 2025 with an allotted time of three years to complete."

"And so, all we have left are the nuclear submarines?" the Prime Minister enquired and continued. "I take it that we in the United Kingdom have kept to schedule and the Russians have not; is that correct?"

"With satellite coverage, we thought that it was possible to check on the integrity of the agreeing parties Prime Minister!"

"But this report; this intelligence report says that the Russians have their nuclear arsenal intact!"

"They didn't keep to schedule, and although under the agreement there were consequences for default on schedule the Russians have since had a regime change." the Foreign Secretary spoke up.

"Intelligence reports have been wrong before," the Prime Minister spoke hopefully.

"Sir, I must protest, we are talking about MI5 and MI6 here!" the Home Secretary retorted.

The Prime Minister looked a little nervously towards the red telephone sitting in front of him. "I spoke to the Russian Ambassador, and he tells me that the President has affirmed that he will not commit an act of war against the British people."

"A phoney war! That is my conclusion," another of the cabinet spoke up.

The Prime Minister responded immediately with some anger in his voice. "There has never been a phoney war, there isn't one; there's no such thing! A phoney peace, perhaps; but never a phoney war!"

Another voice at the table sounded, "The Prime Minister is right. Mankind has always been at a state of war with each other. Yes, we trade, we barter, but our differences are enormous right the way through from birth and unto the promise of good Gods and good Kings!"

The telephone rang three times before the Prime Minister picked the receiver up. Within seconds, he put the telephone down.

"The Russians have just given us two months to evacuate London, Salisbury and Winchester!" There was silence in the room for a full minute before anyone spoke.

"Can't the International community do anything?" the Home Secretary pleaded.

"The International community are under fire, Jeremy! Don't forget that this new Russia have wiped out three European cities in less than three months!" the Prime Minister answered abruptly. He then took off his spectacles, picked up his pipe and walked back towards the window, he then turned around to face the cabinet.

"Right, that's it, we move to the Cabinet War Rooms in London and get all of the chiefs of staff to rendezvous there at the earliest possible time. I want everything up and running with immediate effect."

On the way back to London, the Prime Minister just sat back in the back of the car he was being driven in; he was almost slumping in his seat which prompted the driver to ask how he was feeling; he didn't answer. The Prime Minister knew that the ultimatum was unprecedented in human history. He had been told by the Russians to evacuate London, Salisbury and Winchester within two months; how he asked himself was he going to tell the house and the British people that these cities were to be bombed out of existence by the Russians as a gesture of their power. The questions that he asked himself were absurd at first: "Would they use nuclear bombs to destroy their cities and what of the people who refused to move? He might have to call in the Army; what did he mean might? He had no alternative. That much he did know." In the sixty-five years that he had been alive, he had witnessed a worldwide economic decline that saw in a rationalisation of defence requirements and such that the surface fleet had been greatly diminished; the army fared just as badly and it was hardly worth talking about the air force which had been reduced to about six squadrons of operational aircraft; he knew that they cost so much to develop and build nowadays with what the new Russia investing heavily in an arms race behind closed doors; it had been impossible to keep up with the new Russian developments, and their only recourse was to invest in a second strike capability in the guise of nuclear armed submarines; that was their deterrent against an unforeseen enemy for the opposition in the house and the a large segment of the general public had been lulled into a false sense of security by Russian propaganda. The media hadn't helped matters but that was understandable given the fact that the Oligarchs from the new Russia had managed to acquire major shareholdings in the leading media companies. They had become media moguls and the Prime Minister knew that the strategy of the new Russia was to concentrate their wealth in the hands of 'Oligarchs' who had moved throughout the 'Western World' and with the instructions to wrest control of the capitalist economy of the West. They had been successful, for successive governments had been negligent in relinquishing too much power to the corporations that now held sway over the global economy. As he was thinking, the car drove on and he reached 10 Downing Street late at night.

The following morning the Prime Minister was reviewing a strategy document that had been submitted by one of his cabinet colleagues. The document preferred to lobby all members of the United Nations and with the prospect of isolating the new Russia but the Prime Minister knew that it would be to no avail. He came to an excerpt that nobody had brought to any governments attention in the past and in the present, it ranked with the worst and direst of revelations.

"As you know, there have never been any provisions in any agreement that allows for a change in regime. They, this new Russian Confederation, have not broken Article 23 of the agreement; how could they have? They didn't exist until their regime change. In short, the new Russia was never party to the Nuclear Non-Proliferation Treaty, albeit, true to say that it had been signed by their predecessors."

The Prime Minister put the paper aside, took off his spectacles and wiped his brow with a handkerchief that looked like it had seen better days. He looked at the handkerchief turning its corners in his hand as if knowing that everything was sliding towards an abyss that might well see the end of a United Kingdom. Quite abruptly the phone rang. He picked up the receiver and began to listen.

"I am at the Admiralty, Prime Minister, and the Lord of the Admiralty has told me that he has a plan that just might be successful in thwarting the strategy of this new Russia, it involves a 'Research and Development Project' which is fast coming to completion; he has great hopes for it. We do know now that the previous Russian regime had relinquished their land based nuclear arsenal and were just left with the formidable nuclear submarine fleet that we now face. Prime Minister, the Lord of the Admiralty has assured me that we might be successful in identifying the whereabouts of all Russian Confederation nuclear submarines that have been deployed in the Northern hemisphere; now that would give us an edge, wouldn't it?"

*****

At eleven o'clock the following morning, the Prime Minister left 'Number Ten Downing Street' to rendezvous with the Chiefs of Staff at the Cabinet War Rooms. The House of Commons was not in session and he had decided not to recall members of parliament for debate knowing full well that such a move would only confuse matters. He had decided on one last throw of the dice before committing the country to a subjugation that would see the United Kingdom dissolved and then incorporated in a new and bigger Russian Confederation. Only the cabinet knew about the threat to London, Salisbury and Winchester. He didn't want to cause panic and had decided to keep this information away from prying ears.

At that precise time, Eleanor woke from the deepest sleep she had had for a long, long time. As she awoke, she remembered parts of a vivid dream where she had been placed in a position of repose and in a house full of important people; one of whom was the Prime Minister. Eleanor tried to remember the dream but could only recall parts of it. One thing she did remember, it was the sight of a **'Blue Black Raven'** seemingly towering above her whilst on the other side of a casement window. During the day, bits of the dream came back to haunt her although she could make no sense of any of it yet she did ask herself if there was going to be war.

Chapter 7
Dreams and Whispering Sleeps

"I, Chulyin, Shaman of the North, fly and swim and breathe amongst the mediums of all of life's airs and all of life's waters. Time is my preside, and I count time as it beats the breast that covers the heart for all of life's time is counted this way, and yet man's consensus counts the time taken for the tilted earth to travel around the sun, and the time for the earth to spin on its tilted axis below the silver moon which render him to sleep in dark night and give four seasons winter, spring, summer and autumn to every corner of the earth, and takes the tides on ebbs and floods that wash life ashore and back into the deep from whence all life came forth until the 'Whale' became the Wolf and the Wolf became man until man became man again and again and again. Yet man does not count the infinite realty of time as it beats in the breast of the Whale, the Deer, the Honeybee, the Hummingbird, the Hawk and the Raven; such are my domains as I travel far and wide and here and yonder and adrift on the wind of time always watching and seeking the pathways of the Gods, and I, Chulyin, Shaman of the North, can make happen solutions and within the dominions of dreams and within whispering sleeps that capture all of the imagination's domains."

"I, Chulyin, Shaman of the North, watch as all of beautiful life unfolds and in glorious photonic light; the light given to embryonic life by the Gods who share all of the mountains, skies and seas on earth. I watch life in all its abundance, and I watch still as the embryonic fauna unfolds with all of five senses: touch and taste and smell and sight and hearing intact, and all shared amongst the species and as decreed by the Gods who balance all of the senses in evolution's manifest to counter life and death. The owl excels in sight, and the deer excels in hearing, and all the senses are given in unequal measure to all of life so that life can support itself and as decreed by the Gods; such is the balance of life and the measure of the benevolence of the Gods. And so, life travels in time from the precedence of its unfolding and up unto its folding into the pathways of demise again and again and again; all of Earth's life arriving and leaving until reaching with the unexpectant fingers of life, the transitions and thresholds that all spirits reach. And I watch until all of man's wishes reach the zeniths of inevitable capitulations and the ever present promises of floundering hope that lie before the final setting sun of the lush pastures of all memories which hide the joyous and blissful births, and all of the trials of life and all preside with the recriminations of regret that fester like rough putrid sores on the minds of all who have transgressed against the wishes of the Gods. But all life is in danger of dying now, and I, Chulyin, Shaman of the North, can watch and make happen solutions and within the dominions of dreams and within whispering sleeps that capture all of the imaginations domains."

"I, Chulyin, Shaman of the North, watch as man tinkers and tarries amongst the pathways of the Gods; he samples the delights of the fruits of the forest and of the fields and of the mountains, streams, rivers and seas of life, yet man pays no heed to the balance of life as he counts his power against the power of another and his wealth against the wealth of another, for man's dominions are lost in sleeping idylls that measure his castles of power and not the fruits of the forests of the fields, of the mountains, streams and rivers and seas of life, and he will continue on until he must, touch and taste and smell and hear and see his final conundrum, for time after time man touches the cradles of life with toxic hands that lay to waste all the prospects of evolution and one by one unto the extinction of the Whale, the Deer, the Honeybee, the Hummingbird and the Hawk and the Raven until all of life goes to carrion which must feed the nutrients of the soil which will once again speak to the Gods, and in askance for permit to burst forth into the sun God's path. Yet man will have disappeared from the earth unless I, Chulyin, Shaman of the North, make happen solutions and within the dominions of dreams and within whispering sleeps that capture all of the imagination's domains."

Chapter 8
The Barents Sea

Some eighty degrees north towards the Arctic circle, Frans Josef land lay to the Northeast, Novaja Semlja lay to the east with Svalbard to the Southwest. Right here, Black Guillemots and Ivory Gulls with black beady eyes flew over the small origami shapes of blue white ice that littered the surface of the ocean, making an attractive scene for any man to contemplate. Beneath the surface of one of the world's last clean rich shallow seas, a bearded seal danced and competed with other fish amidst turbulent but plankton filled subsea currents. Below the surface of the sea, the Cod pursued the Capelin fish and a shoal of Herring chased the Copepods which drifted everywhere in swaying and suspended animations. On the sea floor, King Crabs ardent in their work scurried amongst the deep multi-coloured coral reefs, forests and sponges whilst an enormous, silent, ghosting black shape at least one hundred and eighty metres long darkened the sea floor. Nearly all of the crew on board the Ocean Lady were at this hour asleep below decks. The Captain Angus had left his Navigating Officer Vladimir Vinchenko on the bridge, and it was he who was on watch with Simon.

"All hands firmly tucked up in their bunks, Vladimir," Simon announced.

Vladimir didn't turn to face Simon as he spoke.

"Yes, but I like you to check for me please, Simon; go below decks and check they are in their bunks; I want to be sure."

"Right away, Vladimir!" Simon replied.

Vladimir Vinchenko watched the reflection of Simon disappear down the stairwell that led to the sleeping quarters and from the vista of the bridges window to the outside world of the Barents Sea. It was at the precise moment that Eleanor woke up that Simon's head disappeared from view, that all hell broke loose. The Ocean Lady slipped over on to her port side and almost capsized as another enormous vessel almost collided with her; the vessel that pulled right alongside in this Arctic night was a Russian Nuclear Submarine. Below decks on Ocean Lady, the claxon sounded, and as sea water cascaded into the living quarters. Simon had been knocked off his feet and found himself guzzling what seemed like a gallon of seawater; somewhere above him, he heard the screams and shouts of his colleagues and fellow scientists. Eleanor was the first to shout out, 'Oh my God! Are we sinking?' It seemed to be a light year before the Ocean Lady righted herself, and Simon had only just recovered himself as a huge banging noise was heard from the starboard side of the hull. It was then that all of the crew who were sleeping below decks heard the Professor's voice.

"Life jackets on everyone; Vinchenko, Vinchenko, Angus, where are you Angus?"

It was right at that moment that the Ocean Lady's lights went out leaving all crew members in the dark waiting for the next crashing noise to throw them off their feet. "Move everybody! Quickly, up to the bridge!" a voice shouted out from the darkness of the cabin deck and just as lights started to flicker on and off, frightening everyone on board. Eleanor and the Professor were up on the bridge first.

"What in God's name has happened Vladimir?" the Professor implored.

"We were hit by a submarine; it must have been surfacing on to our position!" the navigating officer answered.

The Professor noticed that both Peter the photographer and Vladimir Vinchenko, the navigating officer, had their life jackets on.

"Shall I deploy the life raft?" Vinchenko asked from the Professor.

"I'll make that decision!" a voice came out from the stairwell; it was Angus, the captain, as he emerged onto the bridge with blood streaming down the side of his head. Angus immediately rang the engine room to find out if Ocean Lady was still water tight. He put the communications phone down quickly and addressed everyone on the bridge.

"Right, we have taken on a bit of water but the pumps are working so we should be alright, but it's certain for our trip, I'm afraid, we have lost a lot of fuel."

There was only one word from the Professor, "Damn!"

*****

The young black and white Killer Whale had exceeded the expectations of its pod by singlehandedly despatching the harp seal as it nonchalantly posed on the beach for its mate. The six-tonne mammal beached itself and time and time again by virtually surfing close to the shore right up until it could grab at the harp seal that seemed oblivious to its expectant demise right up until the moment of attack. Having devoured most of the harp seal, the young Killer

Whale was on her way back to her pod which were somewhere offshore of Novaja-Semlja, a large land mass in the Barents Sea leaving the remains of the once light grey harp seal to the common guillemots, the little auks and razorbills that flocked over the remnants of what was once a life form. A million years or more of evolution had bestowed upon the Killer Whale the title of apex predator of the oceans and this one had already demonstrated her abilities by feasting on very large squid at depth and many nautical miles south of this domain. Now travelling beneath the waves, this particular Orca made a communicative sound for her pod even though, they were some thirty nautical miles away; it was a form of echolocation that was used for both hunting and communication and she was listening; listening to every sound in the water which came from every direction at once with underwater sonar which was so sophisticated that she could pick up the movement of absolutely everything at depth. It was in the near vicinity that her sensory brain picked up the movement of the leviathan and in response she emitted a high frequency screech, and then by listening to the alteration of the sound that she had emitted, the young Killer Whale also detected a decibel signature that she was familiar with; it was prey.

*****

They were on their way back to Southampton and Eleanor was again fast asleep. Ordinarily, there is no passion that takes you to a sleep, no deliberation, nor impetus to carry you on a journey but this evening, the unconscious mode of sleep that Eleanor enjoyed carried her into a vivid escapade way beneath the waves and surface of a sea which she seemed to recognise well, indeed everything about her environment was familiar to her

83

through acoustic interpretation alone and not by virtue of the sight of the eye or by virtue of any transmission of light, for the spectrum had been filtered to a dark blue at the depth she was at. The life form that Eleanor was conscious in was in fact another being. Everything in the sea rushed by at speed as the life form detected the leviathan; she immediately let out a high frequency screech which filled the medium with sound, a medium within which the life form veritably sailed. As it traversed its environment, it listened to sounds that the life form had made and was in the process of interpreting every minor and major interruption to the chords that it had emitted into its environment, for the sound that it had emitted was a form of music. All other life in the sea by virtue of being; altered the same chords and this enabled the life form to acoustically read the presence of everything in its environment and in gyroscopic fashion. The life forms huge brain allowed it to see in every direction at once and it was sound reading, not sight reading. The density which prevailed in Eleanor's medium for expression, the water of this vast ocean that she was in, sufficed to provide for a testing domain in which to navigate and to locate the whereabouts of her prey; there were also differing currents and tides with which she was negotiating. These currents and tides had factorial tendencies which could affect the life forms performance, the 'Coriolis' affect, caused by the earth's rotation was but one, yet, evolution had provided this 'Species of Being' with differing types of ailerons, each of which was adapting and enabling efficient and fast travel within the entire domain; Eleanor was reaching speeds of up to fifty kilometres per hour which found her betwixt amazement and deep concentration. The being's eyesight was for the surface and it was almost sight blind at the depths which light could not penetrate yet, the life form was endowed with sophisticated 'hydro acoustic' capability that allowed it to see by sound alone. Quite suddenly, Eleanor became aware of a decibel signature travelling at an alternate angle to her being, and what must have been some seven kilometres away. Eleanor immediately accessed a data memory bank deep within the recesses of her brain, and identified this sound as the prey. Eleanor's auditory sensory capabilities were much faster than the speed at which this decibel signature travelled through the medium, which enabled her being to react at much faster speed. The interception would not be achieved by stealth, on the contrary, for deep within Eleanor's brain were axiomatic reasoning capabilities which equated to the laws pertaining to the very zenith of logic and mathematical computation; these being both geometric and trigonometric, and evolution had also provided the life form with 'geodetic navigational methodology' entirely specific for the geometry and hyperbolic nature of its environment. Within seconds of receiving the decibel signature, her mind had instigated 'frequency spectral masking' which eliminated auditory interference from both the environment that it was travelling in and any other life in the ocean that Eleanor was swimming in. Simultaneously, the being that Eleanor was inhabiting began to compute the distance and position of her prey and by calculating the angles necessary for rendezvous by the use of trigonometry. Eleanor's new being first deduced a tangent angle, then a cosine angle, and then hypotenuse after hypotenuse, and as Eleanor's being sailed through a medium of constantly changing currents, the life form constantly revised all calculations until finally calculating the sine of the angle which would identify the direction necessary for attack. The scientific methodology used enabled Eleanor to zone in on a prey which was only marginally inferior to herself, and she arrived at the rendezvous point less than ten minutes after she had received a decibel indication which had travelled towards her being at over fifteen hundred metres per second. But at precisely four o'clock in the morning and before any other event could unfold, she awoke from the most vivid dream that she had ever had.

*****

On the way back to Southampton, and as they were approaching port and their moorings at the Oceanographic Institute, the Professor, Eleanor and Simon watched from the bridge deck as dolphins raced before the bow of the boat seemingly dancing before the bow waves that were being created by the movement of Ocean Lady.

"They are beautiful creatures, aren't they, Simon?" Eleanor shouted above the noise of the engines and the waves which were thrashing the sides of the hull.

"They most certainly are!" Simon answered, taking a close look into Eleanor's eyes.

Eleanor looked right back at Simon. "I'll bet you didn't know that Orcas are part of the same family!"

"I wasn't aware of that, Eleanor," and he quite suddenly put his arm around Eleanor's shoulder and drew her close to him touching his head against hers as he did so.

Eleanor then tucked her head onto Simon's chest and rested it there until the Professor spoke.

"It's a pity that we haven't got the data we wanted to get, isn't it, Simon?" Eleanor said whilst tucking one of her hands inside Simon's unzipped waterproof jacket.

The Professor was trying to listen to them from a distance of some feet and found it necessary to spoil their first amorous encounter.

"You're wrong there, Eleanor; I checked all of the equipment this morning. Someone had left the sonar on, and the spectrograph was running; we'll check on it all when we get back to port!" he shouted.

It was Eleanor that noticed the **Arctic Tern**; it had perched itself on one of the aft hatches and away from the attention of the salt water spray which coated Ocean Lady almost entirely. Eleanor watched it closely as it fluffed up its feathers as if trying to blanket itself from the cold arctic air. They came back to the same spot time and time again to see if the bird had gone, but it never moved an inch over the entire journey home, moving Simon to make many jokes about its whereabouts.

"I'll bet it's lost, Eleanor!"

Simon had spoken those words on more than one occasion, but for Eleanor there was something eerie about its presence on board; she had noticed an **Arctic Tern** earlier in the trip, and whilst they were on their way in to the Barents Sea; she was sure it was the same bird but felt that she was just being silly in thinking along those lines. On one occasion, Eleanor had been left alone on deck by Simon who was feeling the icy arctic wind on his body and had gone down to fetch his protective coverings, and whilst he did so the bird flew the small distance towards Eleanor and stopped on the deck not three feet away. Eleanor watched the bird as it twisted its head from side to side taking a good look at her, and it continued to do so for a full ten minutes and up until Simon reappeared on deck; then it seemed to lift and float upon the wind until it landed back to its repose on the hatch. Throughout the journey home Eleanor would go back to the aft deck, and on occasions noticed that it had gone, but it always returned and right up until Ocean Lady saw landfall.

Chapter 9
The Lieutenant Commander

Lieutenant Commander James Carmichael, stood on his own patio and looked towards his garden when his daughter popped her head out of the garden shed and asked both his wife Jean and him if they wanted a show. They both laughed together. It was a beautiful, sunny day, but he found himself preoccupied with the mounting political tensions between the West and the Russians. He was a serving Royal Navy Officer and knew that his primary and foremost obligation was to take orders from above, but nobody was exempt from learning of the political and diplomatic discussions taking place at the United Nations. The United Kingdom he knew had, along with their American allies, been having trouble with the Russians ever since the Middle East had blown up into the very debacle it now was. Like so many of his fellow officers there was to do and if necessary, die defending the nation.

His wife Jean spoke first. "What are we in for here, Darling; I wonder?"

"Is it the bowling with my cricket stumps or the juggling, Oh, it is the juggling; we are in for a treat; let's see if she can still perform," he replied.

His daughter came closer carrying a small bag of tennis balls, she took out five of them and started to juggle. "Look Daddy, ET. I'm ET!"

"Oh, those wonderful Americans, what will they teach you next?"

"Don't you like ET, Daddy?" his daughter shouted back.

"I love him, I absolutely love ET!" he shouted back.

They could have been watching an artisan in Covent Garden performing; his daughter hadn't forgotten a trick that he had taught her. David was enjoying the afternoon immensely, but it was during the six o'clock news that he had the warning. Russia had been suspended from the UN's Security Council. He listened briefly to the news and specifically to the report. After the report had ended, his wife, with a worried look on her face, asked a question.

"The news report mentioned NATO's DEFCON system; what does 'DEFCON' mean, darling?" his wife, Jean, had raised her voice.

The Lieutenant Commander did not answer, but he knew fully that 'DEFCON 2' was the result of serious equations that perfectly described beginnings and outcomes from a military perspective. DEFCON was always initiated by politicians, but NATO had devised the system for strategic and tactical comprehension, and in order to advise Allied governments, accordingly. Lieutenant Commander Carmichael knew what DEFCON 2 meant. It sounded loudly in his mind. *High readiness; armed forces ready to deploy in six hours.*

"Do the Russians mean war, Darling, do they?" but before he could answer his wife he heard the telephone in the conservatory ringing.

At 7:30 that evening, David Carmichael tucked his daughter in; it was always his wish to tell her one of his own stories before she slept, and this evening was no different.

"Tell me about the snow leopard, Daddy, please tell me about the snow leopard, Daddy; they are still here, aren't they?" his daughter implored and then shouted, "You be the snow leopard, Daddy!"

"Alright, alright, I'll tell you all about the snow leopard and then you go off to sleep!" David Carmichael began to tell a story before his daughter went to sleep, and just as he had always done when he was at home.

It is cold, but I do not feel the cold. I am at a height of twelve thousand feet, and my being has changed. I am no longer a human being but a snow leopard of about two feet high at the shoulders and six feet long, but my weight, of nearly one hundred pounds, does not inhibit my progress as I crouch on all fours, slowly creeping forward in a halting manner in order to remain hidden. My whitened soft-grey coat with ringed spots of brown help camouflage me from the prey which I have tracked by virtue of my acute sense of smell, and the tracks that my target had made in the snow. My terrain is a steep cliff on the side of a mountain which has rocky outcrops and ravines; a prohibitive domain for all, but the intrepid of any species. My prey is a wild mountain goat, it is only fifty feet away, and it is still oblivious to its plight. Readying myself for the ambush, I open my light green eyes wider in order to let in all of the light that was available in this snow, dusted early morning, and just as the goat moved its head from side to side as if sensing that it was being hunted. Far above, the noises of an aircraft bristles my fur, I watch briefly as it leaves white linear smoke trails in the sky, and it moves me to crouch even lower on large padded paws which had left silent tracked impressions on the snow laden mountainside. Within a flash of movement, I propel myself forwards by the use of powerful hind limbs; I leap upwards and over the

craggy rock face towards the unsuspecting mountain goat;
I close the distance in second ...Oh no, he's got away!

"Did he get away, Daddy, I'm glad. I didn't want you to catch that poor Billy goat..." It wasn't long before his daughter had fallen asleep. At four o'clock exactly, David Carmichael slipped quietly out of bed, walked to his daughter's bedroom and took a lasting look at his child who was sleeping soundly. Careful not to wake his wife, he grabbed his uniform from the closet in his own bedroom and closed the door behind him. Creeping silently down the stairs, he decided to start writing something for his wife; he would finish it at the base, and just in case something happened to him. He sat at his desk in his office and began to write.

"Darling Jean,
I am sorry to be leaving your side at such short notice. I was so looking forward to spending more time with you. It seems that we, in the United Kingdom, are in conflict yet again and not from our making..."

David Carmichael didn't finish his letter, indeed, he crumpled it into a small round ball and placed it in his pocket; there were no words which could describe how much he loved his wife Jean, and he had reminded himself that as a serving officer he shouldn't elaborate upon the world of politics. At five in the morning, Lieutenant Commander Carmichael was back on duty; he placed his bag with his uniform and other clothing into the boot of his car and walked quickly to the driver's side. As he opened the door to get in, he looked up at the drawn curtains which assured him that both his wife and his daughter were still asleep, he hadn't made a sound as he left to rendezvous with the yard. Unbeknown to his family, he would be away for months at the very least, for he knew that his first obligation was to complete the testing of a revolutionary design in sonar detection. He was unaware that amongst the branches of his garden Oak, which hid their house from the road, silently hid a **'Blue Black Raven'** that had been perched there all day and into this early morning light; as the car drove out of the driveway the Raven hopped from one branch to another before lifting its wings to fly off towards the moon.

*****

The Lieutenant Commander was not satisfied with the progress made so far, but he knew that it was all experimental; the problem was with the data base, and for that they relied heavily upon the survey ships with the newly fitted ultra-sensitive hydrophones. His mind wandered a little further forward to the deployment of his facility and in a safe and secure environment, but of course, he was well aware that they had to hide from prying ears and the Russians, he knew, were difficult playmakers. He had managed to convince the Ministry of Defence to fund further development of the sonar suite, and now they were up and running and ready for testing. He was to put it mildly disappointed, for he knew they just weren't ready. They had yet to fine tune the system; access to all of the instrumentation was a problem, and he knew that they would not be able to identify the whereabouts of the Russian nuclear submarines, and at four in the morning, he found himself in his quarters; listening to the admiral in charge of the research and development programme whilst on the telephone. The Lieutenant Commander was explaining the problems to him.

"Yes, I realise that we only have one minute to intercept a submarine – launched ballistic missile, Admiral!"

"Yes, but the trouble is that the new survey ships have only been operating for six months. Although, it is as you say a fact that the new hydro-phonic and photographic recorders are working well. We just need more time to annotate the data base; we need more data, Admiral!"

"Yes, I did propose an alternative. It entailed the deployment of subsea hydro-phonic and photographic recorders, but budget was the prohibiting factor, and anyway, the risk analysis clearly showed that retrieval at serious depth would be nearly impossible." The conversation went on for an hour.

The new sonar equipment, named Skana, together with the instrumentation which was to be placed on board HMS Moment included a silicon orb which showed the boat at the centre of the orb. The direction-finding capability was affected by using a new geodetic referencing map which had been evolved by inversing the Mercator projection techniques used for surface navigation. The orb room with the 'Inverse Mercatorial View' was immense and filled the whole of the broadest part of the mock up hull which was to be the forehead section of the ship. Lieutenant Commander Carmichael donned his protective suit and walked in upon a walkway to a control station, set at the centre of the orb. In this centre was an array of instrumentation that showed readings of sonar signals both high and low frequency; all of them were attempting to identify objects beneath the surface of the sea. The new instrumentation was so sensitive that it could pick up the smallest of frequencies, and the orb identified the direction from which the reading was coming from. Automatic switches on the console lit up points of interest and their distance from the ship.

Once the equipment was switched on, the central console displayed points of topographical interest; shoals of fish and cetaceans and all other movements beneath the sea came to life.

"What is this one here at Latitude 50 degrees 35 minutes, Longitude 20 degrees 16 minutes, 35.4 nautical miles?" the Lieutenant Commander asked as he pointed to a screen on the central console.

"We're not sure as yet, Sir, we keep getting fluctuating readings!" the crew member answered.

"Well, what do they tell us?" he asked abruptly and a little impatiently.

"We're getting three readings at the same location, Sir; they're fluctuating between a shoal of fish, a cetacean and topographical features, I'm afraid."

"Damn it!" the Lieutenant Commander exclaimed.

*****

The director of engineering; a robust looking man in his early fifties stood within the construction shed talking above the noise and clamour of a very busy workshop indeed.

"Yes, we have three boats under construction at the moment and boat two; your boat will be the only boat fitted with the new sonar suite; it looks quite impressive, Sir."

The lieutenant commander, watched as the giant trolley system began to move the forehead section towards the completed part of the boat. The Lieutenant Commander spoke first.

"You asked, so I'll tell you; the sonar reference position of target or points of interest by taking an 'Inverse Mercatorial View' of the area of interest which can be approximately two hundred miles in every direction, so what you see on the command deck is the inside of an orb which is segregated into longitudinal and latitudinal positions. I've tested everything, and it should now work perfectly; there are a couple of problems that are to be ironed out, but I am sure that the sea trials will prove that all is well with the sonar suite."

The director of engineering smiled wryly and pointed out at one of the young apprentices to the Lieutenant Commander before telling him what had had to be completed.

"Well, as you know, it took the team six months to alter the design on boat two, so that we were completely satisfied that all was well with the incorporation of the new sonar suite. The change to the design was one of the most advanced technological projects we have ever undertaken because we had to alter virtually every control layout on the command deck; there are almost eight million components. The back of the boat is taken up by the nuclear reactor, the engines, which are steam turbines, and of course the backup systems; and as you can see, we have finished installation there, and we are ready to start manoeuvring the forehead section of the hull with your new sonar suite on board on Sunday. It will take eight welders working day and night shifts for three weeks, and then we have to hook up and test." Lieutenant Commander Carmichael was looking forward to be submersed in the submarine.

"Incidentally, how long can the boat spend underwater?" the Lieutenant Commander asked.

"Well, as I have said the nuclear reactor will last for thirty years or more but the crew will not, so until such time as we can facilitate all that we need from the subsea environment we are restricted to about four months; after that time we replenish," came the reply.

During the week that followed, the boat was undergoing final construction and was being readied for its sea trials; they were all hoping that the boat, HMS Moment, would be ready for deployment and active service almost as soon as it had completed them. The sea trials were scheduled to start the following month and Lieutenant Commander Carmichael and his team were all working overtime to install the latest analysis software into the onboard computer; he and two of HMS Moment's other ratings were spending equal time in the boat's simulator. The trials which they were all about to embark on encompassed the testing of the new hydrophone system and testing of the latest torpedoes and ballistic missiles which could be better guided on to the respective targets. The nuclear reactor which broke down the uranium for fuel, was also to be tested again and whilst at sea. He was to give a talk on the new sonar suite before they set out for sea trials; that was how tight the schedule was. Lieutenant Commander David Carmichael lifted the cup and saucer in front of him up and began to gently stir. It was Earl Grey, he liked Earl Grey, but quite suddenly the door burst open and a chief petty officer stood there.

"I'm sorry to intrude, Sir, but you have been ordered to report to the Admiralty in London, immediately!"

The commander then carefully put the cup and saucer down, took his jacket from its peg on the back of the door and left the office. The last thing he did as he left the building was to polish the Royal Navy Officers badge on his hat. At approximately 12:30 the following day, Lieutenant Commander Carmichael had been given the instruction to liaise with an MI5 officer at the Oceanographic Institute in Southampton, and at a time when not one person, outside of the cabinet or the Ministry of Defence, were aware of the looming crisis.

Chapter 10
The Oceanographic Institute

Annabelle had done her homework well; she had read all there was to know about 'Cetacean Warfare Programs', and all about the 'Kazachya Bukhta' research facility near Sevastopol; the Russian facility that specialised in the use of marine mammals for military purposes. Russian personnel were at the top of her list, and she had, with the help of MI6, located the whereabouts of all strategic Russian personnel barring two; Annabelle had their details and photographs. She had also read up on the Oceanographic Institute and had ensured that all of their personnel's incoming and outgoing professional and personal communications were being monitored. Eleanor was looking ahead to the upcoming meeting with the Professor at the Oceanographic Institute when the phone rang.

"Good morning, Annabelle speaking."

Annabelle listened to the call and then just said thank you; she then put the phone down. The phone call had provided her with her itinerary for the day; she was to meet with Lieutenant Commander Carmichael at the Oceanographic Institute in Southampton; they were, she had been told, being expected.

*****

Another evening had come to its end, and Eleanor was yet again getting ready for bed. The morning was, in her estimation, going to be fraught with difficulty; she was worried; worried that the government, who had told them all at the Oceanographic Institute that they would be arriving and with no ceremony, might close the program down. As she turned the bedside table light out, Eleanor placed her head upon a sumptuous pillow and immediately started to fall into sleep. Time went by, but the awakening that she had not been looking forward to was preceded by another, for yet another vivid dream state awoke her first. Eleanor was flying high above the parapets of buildings on thoroughfares that bled the choking traffic fumes. Eleanor wasn't alone for milling, all around her were other black and white and just pure white seagulls of every kind, and all making the squawking sounds that seemed to echo on and off a wind that carried her being in every conceivable direction. At first, she was ascending and then descending, Eleanor was now a master of the cloudy, blue-grey sky as she drifted on high, and then with a deftness that surprised her mind she crafted her wings, so that she fell sixty feet or more onto a pavement without so much as even the slightest shock to her frame. Hovering on gifted wings, Eleanor balanced her being upon the air whilst surveying the street scene, and then just as quickly turned full circle; seemingly climbing up slowly an invisible staircase that led to a higher vantage point. Down she swooped again and flew at speed along a thoroughfare that led to a row of yachts all tied to a jetty; she skirted around ratlines that ching-changed their familiar metallic sounds upon the wind. Eleanor landed on a burnt umber, hardwood jetty; a man was clambering up a short gangplank, and she recognised him immediately; it was Peter, the Canadian photographer; she could even read the name on the stern of the yacht; it read 'Sojourn' Southampton. The man named Peter turned, but there was no familiar smile; only a stern demeanour greeted her stare, and then suddenly she was awake, sweating and staring into the abyss of a darkened room. Eleanor was terrified as the look in the Canadian's eyes seemed to give her a premonition of death.

*****

At ten o'clock in the morning, the Professor was sitting at his desk waiting for his visitors to call in on him; he wondered what it could be about and was procrastinating with Simon who had suggested that sonar might just be construed by the Royal Navy to be a sensitive subject.

"We are talking civilian here and scientific; since when the military had the right to interfere with civilian programs?" the Professor complained.

Eleanor was frowning, "You did report the incident of the Russian submarine to the authorities, Professor; they might just want to talk about the incident!" Eleanor spoke up.

"I am just a little worried, that's all; you know we have identified something on the spectrograph, if it is the Russian submarine then they might want to intrude upon the program," the Professor replied.

The small group of Marine Scientists didn't have long to wait. Within minutes there was a knock at the door and the Professor's secretary poked her head around the opened door.

"Your guests are here, Professor; shall I let them in?" The Professor just nodded and stood up behind his desk. Even though they were expecting a Royal Navy Officer, he,

Eleanor and Simon were surprised to see Lieutenant Commander Carmichael standing in front of them wearing full uniform. The Lieutenant Commander took his hat off, walked straight towards the Professor and proffered his hand.

"Good morning Professor, I've brought someone with me from the Home Office, this is Annabelle," he said whilst ushering her forward to meet the group.

"Did you have a good trip down?" the Professor asked.

"Yes, thank you," came the reply, which was neither perfunctory nor abrupt which rather surprised him; he was expecting an authoritarian voice at first greeting.

"Well, Professor, Annabelle here is from the Home Office and we have come to hear all about this run in that you had with the Russian nuclear submarine! Can you tell us about the incident?"

Eleanor pulled up two chairs for them to sit on.

"Well, there is nothing much to tell really, only that we were all asleep in our bunks at the time," the Professor announced whilst demonstrating his level of commitment to the proceedings.

"So nobody got a look at the submarine? Was there anyone on the bridge at the time?"

"Well, yes there was actually; Viktor Vinchenko, our navigating officer; he was on watch."

"And at the helm!" Annabelle put in.

The Professor took a long cold look at Annabelle and then tried to ignore her.

"Yes he was," Simon replied.

"Can we talk to Viktor?" Annabelle asked.

"I'm afraid not, after the accident he went off on leave."

Annabelle reached into her shoulder bag and pulled out a buff envelope. She then went straight over to the

100

Professor's desk and laid a photograph on the table. "Is this Viktor Vinchenko?"

The Professor stared at the photograph momentarily and then picked it up from the desk. "Yes it is!" he answered and then whilst taking a long look into Annabelle's eyes, he asked a question.

"Why, is there a problem?"

"Well yes there is I am afraid; his name is not Victor Vinchenko. MI5 have informed the Home Office that he is a certain Vladimir Koseygin, wanted by the authorities for espionage activities. He is Russian!"

"This is absurd, I've known him for years. Anyway, he's Ukrainian, Angus, our Captain hired him! Anyway, why would the Russians be interested in us?" At that point, Annabelle interrupted the Professor.

"Vladimir Koseygin had years previously been a Russian Navy attaché at the 'Kazachya Bukhta' research facility near Sevastopol; the facility specialised in the use of marine mammals for military purposes!"

"But our programme is only concerned with translating the Killer Whales language!" Eleanor almost shouted.

During this time, Simon had been quietly thinking and watching Annabelle's every gesture; he was sure that she was an MI5 officer but he refrained from suggesting anything of that sort.

"Is this all to do with sonar?" he asked.

"Have you been working on Orca's sonar, Professor, because if you have I should be terribly interested in how far you have got with your scientific enquiry?" the Lieutenant Commander asked.

"I need to know where this so-called Viktor Vinchenko has gone, Lieutenant Commander; as you are aware it's terribly important that the authorities apprehend him." "Oh,

I am sorry, Annabelle; I'll leave it to you for the time being."

"Does anyone know where Viktor Vinchenko might be?"

There was then a stony silence in the room.

"You are probably unaware of this, but the Home Office believe that you were all in danger of losing your lives."

The Professor's mouth dropped open as he looked straight at Annabelle.

Annabelle then produced another photograph; it was of Peter, their Canadian photographer. "Is this man on your staff too, Professor?"

The Professor looked shocked; he took off his spectacles and picked the picture up.

"There was a murder in Canada, Professor, and this man is wanted by the Canadian authorities; he is under suspicion of murder; Peter Campbell isn't his real name, I can tell you that much! No, we believe that he too is Russian."

"But I…I… I… wasn't… I mean, I didn't know …." the Professor at that juncture went visibly pale. Both Simon and Eleanor were also shocked into silence.

*****

"How did the Russian submarine know you were in the Barents Sea and at that location; someone must have told them."

Simon spoke up, "You mean the sonar, don't you? Someone had left the sonar on; we didn't know anything about it until we got back to port."

The Lieutenant Commander then addressed everyone.

"If there is any recording of the events then I can tell you right now that that data is now the property of Her Majesty's Government!"

The conversation went on for an hour or more. The Professor talked about the programme, and he could see by the expression on the Lieutenant Commander's face that he was absolutely enthralled. At the end of his talk, the Professor seemed a little down in the mouth.

"I expect that this means the end of our programme!"

"On the contrary, Professor; I think that you are doing something that the whole of mankind will be interested in!" Annabelle spoke up again and rather quickly.

"We are going to have to look at all of your security arrangements because I am afraid to tell you that your programme is now 'Top Secret'!"

"You must understand, Professor; the Russians must have a good reason to investigate your programme. Can you think of anything that might enlighten us?" the Lieutenant Commander asked.

It was right at that juncture that Eleanor spoke up.

"You've found something, Simon; haven't you, on the spectrograph readings?"

Simon seemed a little sheepish but got up and went to the back of the room where another desk stood. On it was a roll of spectrograph data which he had been about to show the Professor.

"I didn't know what this was, but it seems that we were recording Orcas throughout the period that we were steaming in the Barents Sea; of course, there is all of the interference from the Russian Submarine but there was something else."

The Lieutenant Commander looked towards Simon who seemed quite worried. "Don't worry; we are only here to help."

Simon rolled the spectrograph data recording out onto the conference table and pointed to areas on the spectrograph which he had ringed in red ink.

"Orca had transmitted this data which has no premise on any other recording. I think it indicates the whereabouts of that submarine!"

"What?" the Lieutenant Commander shouted out. He rushed to the table and started to ask Simon questions. "How can you be sure Simon? What time was it when Orca sonar pulsed the communication?"

"Well, the time is shown up here. We have been pouring over these recordings of Orca for weeks now, and there have been very few recordings which show this particular type of graphical representation over a forty-year period; of course, we have got a lot better over the last year or so …"

The Lieutenant Commander interrupted Simon before he could utter another word. "Are you sure, Simon?"

"Yes, I am certain; as I said we have looked at the data taken over a forty-year period," Simon answered emphatically, "and on the last occasion, the occasion of the incident, both Orca and the submarine were in range of each other and right at the outset."

Lieutenant Commander Carmichael smiled wryly, "I still don't see how you could have identified that Orca can determine the whereabouts of submarines at depth; tell me how you did it, and I'll listen!"

"We, that is the team and I, used the capacity of public computers that were laying idle in much the same way as SETI does just in order to increase our computing power, and we concentrated that extra computing power on the graphical data shown on the spectrograph. I mean, the initial idea was to completely translate Orca's language, but we have, alas, fallen well short of our target thus far. What we have determined is that Orca communicates at high frequency in sequence. He or she gives location first which is shown here on the spectrograph."

Simon rather enthusiastically pointed to the lines drawn on the spectrographs that identified the Orca's location.

"They follow this up with identification of an object or species or shoal in the water," Simon pointed to the next group of lines in the sequence.

"Are you certain that Orca can verify depth and range of a submarine, Simon?"

"We have proved it just by using mathematics!" Simon returned.

"So, if we can identify this submarine, we can identify them all! What a development!" the Lieutenant Commander exclaimed. "All we have to do is listen in to Orca."

"But we still can't work out in which direction the sonar pulses are coming from, Sir; the most we can determine is a spherical rang and distance; and that means you won't be able to determine the position of any nuclear submarine."

Lieutenant Commander Carmichael walked up to the Professor's desk, "Don't you worry, Professor; the Royal Navy will deal with that particular problem; all you have to do is keep very quiet about this whole affair, but for the time being, I'm afraid it's not business as usual for the Oceanographic Institute, The whole facility is under lockdown until we can instigate more efficient security arrangements."

Chapter 11
The Coming War

Annabelle was sitting behind her desk at Thames House in London. After reading her e-mails, she had set to work on yet another case, another lead in her department's investigations. MI5 were in the process of scouring all communications with the specific aim of isolating any strings of data that would help to identify Russian sponsored insurgents; some of whom may have been alive as spies within the United Kingdom over the past ten years and since the beginning of the Russian military incursions that had been taking place. Of course, Annabelle knew that the general public had been unaware of the good work that all at MI5 did, but that was essential, the public only need to know that the government of the United Kingdom had all in hand. Annabelle was the case officer for the file titled 'Sonar', and she typically continued to work and slept on the subject along with the other duties that had been delegated to her. Her thoughts on this March morning were on the military developments that were right at that moment taking place; all at MI5 were aware of the Russian ultimatum but not one word was spoken in anger; rather there was a quiet determination to assist the military in what was the most serious hour that the United Kingdom had ever faced. The Lieutenant Commander came to Annabelle's mind and on more than one occasion, but it was only when walking her dog on this auspicious morning that she said a silent prayer. The lady she always met on the wooded path would not have known.

The Professor had been silent for days; he hadn't talked to either Eleanor or Simon about the affair that had them all worried even though their fears had been allayed by the lady from the Home Office. In the main, he'd talked to the Lieutenant Commander about his own philosophy and voiced the concerns that he had about nuclear armaments; both he and the Lieutenant Commander agreed to differ. The Professor preferred to believe that mankind should not need nuclear weapons in a day and age that had lines of communication wide open right across the world, but the Royal Navy officer had made it quite plain that he believed in the need for the détente. History, he had said, was strewn with the broken promises of those that had a craving for power. He was, of course, pleased that his visitor was enthralled by the work that they had been doing and had spent a long time talking about mankind's space quest to find extra-terrestrial life; of course, he had talked about Orca and had told the Lieutenant Commander that in his opinion the human race had the same chance of deciphering an alien language when the likelihood was that such life forms may neither think like man nor look anything like man. Everyone had taken leave from work whilst new security arrangements were being put in place, but he couldn't wait to get back to the task of translating whatever he could of the Killer Whale's language, firmly believing that successful translations of the high and low frequency data strings might lead to a form of communication between Orca and man which would be beneficial to the wellbeing of all life on their planet home that mankind had called 'Earth'. It was a cold March day, and he wore his scarf tightly around his neck as he strolled along a promenade in Southampton that was awash with the breaking wave. He was just like the rest of the population, unaware that the crisis being spoken about in muted terms was like no other crisis that the United Kingdom had faced in the past.

*****

At the same time that the Professor had been walking along the promenade, both Simon and Eleanor were sitting in a popular bistro. They were both silent as they tucked in to a welcome lunch; the news was almost being delivered throughout the day and concerned Russian aggression towards the United Kingdom. Both were unaware that serious military business was being counted, after all, the Lieutenant Commander hadn't revealed anything of the sort; he hadn't said much, but his silence when asked questions on the subject matter of Orca's sonar was enough. They were, of course, all ordinary people employed at doing extraordinary things and like so many other people who worked in research and, of course, development and security. Simon was transfixed on Eleanor whom he had fallen in love with, and just like the gentleman he was, his concern was not for himself but for Eleanor. As scientists, they wanted the very best of outcomes for mankind and the environment and had more than once voiced concerns about the Royal Navy's intentions, yet time and time again they remembered the lieutenant commanders last words to them. He had told them that if they were right then the whole of humankind would be the beneficiaries. They believed him, and they believed in the work that they were doing; he had told them to go back to that to work and that they should carry on as normal whilst assuring them that the Royal Navy would put their findings to the very best of use.

Lieutenant Commander David Carmichael walked alongside the water in Regents Park in a state of bewilderment. He had spent the most part of his working life working on acoustic technology, and whilst in 'The Royal Navy' and here, he now was having to conjure up the courage to inform the Prime Minister that all of the Royal Navy's scientific and technological knowhow was rudimentary compared to that of a species of **a** cetacean. He was wondering what the Chiefs of Staff would have to say when he addressed them on the subject of Orcinus orca, the Killer Whale. David Carmichael was feeling the cold and was wearing an overcoat that covered his uniform feeling that it gave him the anonymity that he wanted this cold and icy morning, and he kept looking at his watch, for he was fully aware that at two o'clock in the afternoon he would be in the 'Cabinet War Rooms' consulting with the Chiefs of Staff and the Prime Minister on the methods that he was going to employ to find the Russian nuclear submarines that had all put to sea. All manner of people were walking by, and he knew that all of them were oblivious to the crisis facing the United Kingdom; it was serious and so serious that the government had had to invoke the Emergency Powers Act; they had also curtailed the press and all other media outlets. At a quarter to one, he sat on a bench and stretched his legs out in front of him. To any onlooker, he looked like a man on his lunch break; his hands rested deep in his overcoat's pockets; he was reminded that he had forgotten his gloves that morning; it seemed absurd to him that he should, and at a time like this, remember that his daughter had bought him the gloves for Christmas. He watched people walking by, some talking amongst themselves whilst others sidled to the railings to watch the beautiful white swans that rested silently on the crisp clear water of Regents Park, a park that was once the hunting ground of Henry the Eighth. He began to wonder about nature and about the Killer Whale, Orcinus orca; he wondered what the proponents of the Gaia philosophy would say; perhaps, the earth was indeed a living organism which was in balance with itself after all. A bird flew close to him; it was a **Raven**; he watched the huge **'Blue-Black'** bird as it ambled toward the bench that he was sitting on. Watching the **Raven**, he noticed that the bird was eyeing him by craning its neck from side to side, but just as he was about to throw the bird a piece of bread that was lying in front of him, the bird opened its wings and flew up into the cold morning air. As he watched the Raven fly away, David Carmichael's demeanour changed completely. He had this great feeling of apprehension as he knew that convincing the Chiefs of Staff that they should take an enormous risk by sending a fleet to sea on the justification that he had to offer was going to be difficult. He believed in the Professor's work and had had a long conversation with him whilst they were at the Oceanographic Institute. The Professor had been worried that his work in translating the Killer Whale's language would be used for military purposes, and he, Lieutenant Commander Carmichael of the Royal Navy, had had to convince the Professor that they were only interested in the developments. The détente which would suffice to alleviate the crisis facing the United Kingdom remained secret. The morning had disappeared into an afternoon; the hours had just run past him; he then looked at his watch for the last time before alighting from the bench that he had been sitting on and walked in the direction of a waiting car.

*****

The Prime Minister had been thinking. In his frustration, at the turn of international events, he was wondering where it had all gone astray. He did, of course, know about history, about how 'Nation States' were formed. He knew that they were either born of political or economic bias and Russia, born as it was of an Imperial State had evolved towards being a politically biased Communist State which had since the advent of Bolshevism moved toward international revolution. They had, he knew always, been on the march without counting the dissolution of the USSR which was forced upon 'Mother Russia' by economic circumstance alone. The Prime Minister had also always known that mankind's struggle towards a utopian existence had begun with a striving for power. Communism, he had long since decided, was an ideology devised by mankind, just as some Gods were; and these idioms of power, he had decided, were designed to form the very basis of allegiance in areas of the world where real education had been kept from ordinary people. In the case of the United Kingdom, the people had a parliamentary democracy with the monarch as the 'Head of State', all of whom, and by more than tradition, were beholden to an ecclesiastical homage which would always wear the cloak of progress; such was the power of the learned. But what of the people in these renegade states? Well, he had long since known that a lot of people in a lot of nation states had been hostages to the wrong forms of power right up until the advent of democracy which relied upon mutual respect and understanding between nations and all being fostered through the merchant and international trade. But where, he asked himself, was the international community now, at a time when gods had given way to a new form of power; a most destructive one; nuclear weaponry? And he asked himself the question that had been nagging at him for half a century or more "When will mankind allow itself to pay homage to the individual?" Such was this man; a man no different to any other politician living in a complex world. He had been looking constantly at the clock hanging on the wall of the Cabinet War Room, it was ten minutes to two o'clock, and his secretary had walked in. "They are all here, Sir; the Chiefs of Staff!"

"Right, send them in!" he replied.

The Chiefs of Staff were all sitting down looking towards the Prime Minister when he began to talk.

"As you are all aware, the Russian government are proposing the destruction of the World as we know it for nothing more than a political bias. They have given the government of the United Kingdom the most terrible of ultimatums. This is what we are going to do."

Chapter 12
HMS Vanguard

Lieutenant Commander Carmichael couldn't shake off the enormous feeling of apprehension that had been with him ever since he had been told that he was to set his equipment up on the frigate HMS Vanguard; he knew it was a heavy responsibility, and one that he shared with the team at the Oceanographic Institute. He'd spoken to the Professor, Simon and Eleanor at length, and veritably scoured the data that they had provided him with. Annabelle had gone the minute that Eleanor had revealed the name of the yacht that the Russian spy named Peter Campbell owned. He and Koseygin had been apprehended by the police and detained under two acts of parliament, the Prevention of Terrorism Act and the Emergency Powers Act. The Lieutenant Commander had looked at the data for thirty-six hours; he would have liked to have been able to spend longer at the task, and just to reassure himself that all was as the young man named Simon had said; sadly, there wasn't enough time but his faith in the young man was unstinted. The team at the Oceanographic Institute, he knew, would be required in the future, but all that was to be done now was to help supervise the refit of the frigate HMS Vanguard whilst it was in port at Portsmouth. At this juncture and at three o'clock in the morning, he found himself on board the frigate with the Captain and Commander of the fleet that was to sail into the Northern Hemisphere with the goal of destroying the Russian nuclear submarine fleet. It was, he thought at times, unimaginable, but young Simon and the Professor had assured him time and time again that the readings on the spectrograph, all of which were taken from Orca transmissions, definitely showed nuclear submarines. The Royal Navy had of course taken the precaution of ordering all their submarines back to base, and all were ordered to surface for fear of having them mistaken for Russian vessels; all was ready with the exception of the refit of HMS Vanguard a Royal Navy frigate, which had been delayed by rudimentary testing of the new sophisticated hydrophones. The Lieutenant Commander was praying that they would work. For there would be no time for sea trials, the hour was at hand.

*****

Great steel hawsers that had HMS Vanguard bound to the dockside were slipped, allowing the Royal Navy frigate to leave her moorings but ever so quietly. The grey, cloudy, evening sky hid a frightened moon which dared not to show its luminescence for fear of altering the answered prayers of the crew on board. Stealth was being used, and it was being practised by those that hunt and by those that hide; HMS Vanguard was in a life and death game of hide and seek, and in such a game there were winners and losers. At this juncture, they were about to set sail in search of their prey; the whole of the Russian nuclear submarine fleet which were all in the Northern Hemisphere. Lieutenant Commander Carmichael was on the bridge with the Captain and Commander of the fleet. The captain spoke first whilst eyeing the lieutenant commander's badge. "You look like a fish out of water wearing that Dolphin's badge; have you ever been on a warship before?"

Lieutenant Commander Carmichael continued to stare straight not wishing to show the captain his embarrassment.

"I am afraid to say that I haven't!" came the reply, and he paused before adding, "I also have to admit, I'm getting a little seasick!"

The Captain of HMS Vanguard laughed and smiled wryly towards his number two who stood on the bridge next to him.

As they sailed away from Portsmouth harbour, the Captain and Lieutenant Commander Carmichael talked on their mutual careers. What the Captain of HMS Vanguard told him would stay in his mind forever. He had told him why he wanted to become a member of the armed services.

"Mankind first learnt to keep his family safe whilst hunting for food, then man developed the idea that he needed security, perimeter fences, if you like; then there was defence against predators and finally the development of society. Like you, I chose the role of defence. That's right you know, Commander; without our security and defence there would be no society to speak of, and there would certainly be no democracy!"

*****

The Lieutenant Commander addressed his team.

"You are all going to get a very quick introduction into revision one of the system that we have been developing and learning to operate over the past six months; I'm afraid; all that we have been working on is now obsolete, and we have to use a different system; we are going to be listening to the Killer Whale! It's quite simple, really; we now know that it identifies the whereabouts of Russian submarines, and we can identify location on this spectrograph!" he said standing over a very large piece of plotting equipment. "These Orca's transmit high and low frequency sounds into the ocean environment and receive back what could be described as revised sounds which identify whatever there might be in the deep, at least the scientists at the Oceanographic Institute believe that to be the case; don't worry, I've checked their computations, and I believe that they are correct in their assumptions. We have set up our receiver hydrophones to receive in much the same way as Orca does. Orca's transmission and reception capabilities are spatially gyroscopic and for the benefit of the uneducated among us, that means all round vision by the use of sound waves in water! That gentleman is Orca's sonar for you; it is far more sophisticated than we could ever have imagined!"

*****

Eleanor, Simon and the Professor had had a difficult time; at first they thought that they were to be closed down by the government, but then it appeared that the reason for the presence of the Lieutenant Commander and the lady named Annabelle from the Home Office was to inform them that they had been spied upon by the Russian secret service. They were, of course, still in a state of shock and each day since brought the preoccupation of security arrangements which hitherto had been largely ignored. Annabelle had told them all that their lives had been in danger, and that there was the distinct possibility that there had been an attempt on their lives whilst the Ocean Lady was at sea. So much had happened over the past two weeks that Eleanor had not completely forgotten about her dreams which she had now attributed to the Shaman's promise; that he would take her with him and from time to time. On this particular night, she veritably fell into her bed being almost totally exhausted. Eleanor went to sleep immediately, but it was many hours before her subconscious opened up another world which was familiar to her. It was at the same time that HMS Vanguard had positioned itself deep within the Barents Sea and far above abyssal plains and ridges that were the topography of the sea floor.

*****

The sonar hydrophones had been switched on the moment they had left port; one of the ratings sat with earphones on whilst watching the spectrograph. There was nothing to report.

"Anything yet?" he asked again.

"Nothing, Sir, not a thing!"

"Don't worry, keep at your station; I will be on the bridge with the Captain. I want to be informed the moment that an Orca transmits." The Lieutenant Commander placed his hand on the shoulder of the operator in a comforting manner. "We keep listening, lieutenant. No matter how good or bad the technology is, we can do no more than listen!"

The Lieutenant Commander spoke little whilst on the bridge of HMS Vanguard, but he was immersed in thought; there was, of course, the task ahead, all was in place, and all there was to do was to listen, and if they were successful it would be all in the hands of the Commander, the ship's Captain, a professional man whom he did not know, but that was an irrelevance for the structure of command and orders set a scene of action that would they all hoped deliver the right outcome. Of course, they all thought about

Armageddon; of the pending nuclear strikes which would proceed other nuclear strikes, all of which might herald the end of all of civilisation; yes, all of them, thought about Armageddon, every member of the crew, for theirs was an enormous responsibility which relied upon nothing more than sophisticated hydrophones. From time to time, he thought about his home in Devon where he had played with his daughter on the lawn and where he had sat with his wife of twenty-five years, a woman and lady who had brought him so many gifts; he was rich, for he knew that those gifts brought him a contentment that all the tea in China could not provide.

"The satellite is waiting David, any news?" the Commander and Captain of HMS Vanguard asked.

"I'm afraid there is none as yet," came the reply.

They both looked towards the clock that was ticking; it was precisely forty-five minutes before the hour; the hour that had been set by the Russians for nuclear strikes. The Lieutenant Commander found himself mentally reciting 'The Lord's Prayer'; he had got right up to 'forgive us our trespasses' when a lieutenant opened the door to the bridge.

"We have nothing yet, Sir!"

Lieutenant Commander Carmichael breathed a disappointed sigh and then spoke to the Captain and Commander of the small fleet that had set sail into the Northern Hemisphere.

"What better than to listen to one of God's creatures speaking about its environment whilst using its sophisticated sonar capabilities. Millions of years they have been here; we, on the other hand, have been here for a mere two hundred and sixty thousand years. We listen and pray, that's all we can do!"

Beyond the seagoing transepts of man's technologies, a small ivory gull of brilliant white flew over the ice laden Barents Sea as if looking for a place on which to settle, and only the world of nature watched as it disappeared in a fine misty distance. Just above breaking waves, a lone Orca surfaced and began to move after the ivory gull; it seemed to be jostling with the elements that were keeping it from making headway until quite suddenly it dived below the surface and into the oceanic beyond. On board HMS Vanguard, men and women were thinking privately to themselves; pictures of family members; of children, were littered on bunks; all on board were in pensive mood. The Captain was now in the navigation area with Lieutenant Commander Carmichael.

"We've got very little time left, and they are staying hidden, if we can't find them, I'm afraid it's curtains," the Captain stated.

"What is the deadline again?" the Lieutenant Commander asked.

"0' six hundred hours!" the Captain answered.

"After that, our cities will cease to exist as we knew them!" he continued.

"You mean they'll be reduced to rubble and millions will be killed!" he looked extremely distressed as he spoke.

"What alternative did we have?" the captain enquired of Lieutenant Commander Carmichael.

"There wasn't one!" he replied.

At that very second, a rating came to their side. "The sonar officer is looking for you, Sir!"

Lieutenant Commander Carmichael quickly turned away from the captain and walked into the sonar suite.

*****

Everything in the sea rushed by at speed as Eleanor let out a high frequency screeching noise which filled the oceanic medium with sound; a medium within which the Eleanor veritably sailed. As she traversed its environment, she listened to the sounds that she had made, and was in the process of interpreting every minor and major interruption to the chords that she as the Orca had emitted into the oceanic environment; for the sound that Eleanor had emitted was also being read by her for any interruption. All other life in the sea, by virtue of being; altered the same chords that Eleanor had initially emitted; enabling her to acoustically read the presence of everything in her environment and in gyroscopic fashion. Eleanor was using the Orca's huge brain which allowed it to see in every direction at once; she was sound reading, not sight reading. Back from the depths came resonances which described shoals of fish, other life forms and then there they all were; thirty-five, all in different locations. Eleanor had discovered the whereabouts of steel leviathans which were armed with nuclear missiles. Almost automatically she let out another screeching sound which filled the oceans with sound.

*****

The Lieutenant Commander stood over the computer that was reading from the spectrograph. On the screen, a list of locations described the whereabouts of all thirty-five of the Russian nuclear submarines. The sonar operator called the positions out.

"Beaufort Shelf, East Siberian Shelf, West Greenland Rift Basin, East Greenland Rift Basin, Kara Shelf, Barents Shelf, Laptev Shelf, Amerasian Basin, Chukchi Shelf,

Eurasian Basin. All areas between Canada, Alaska, Russia and Greenland, Sir!"

Ten minutes before the hour the captain of HMS Vanguard signalled to the rest of the fleet; all hands were on action stations as the orders were given. There waited and waited some expectant of a response but time went by. There would be no replies.

Chapter 13
The Shaman Returns Home

The Shaman was somewhere over the Arctic circle and way above the tree line where an Arctic fox moved stealthily over a difficult and snow laden landscape. The grey and blue hues carefully painted by the sun's light barely penetrated through slight snowfall which hung in the air like rich billowing curtains; curtains which were thick with billions upon billions of stellar snow plates which would temporarily blind and hold any man's sight at bay. But this Arctic fox's eyes had been adapted for the terrain in all seasons, winter, spring, summer or autumn, as was his sense of smell which right at this moment had cautioned him to steer away from an ice hole which was somewhere out there in the not too far distance. Despite the snow, black and white Arctic terns swooped by to check on what remained of an already rotted carcass left by Inuit hunters but they soon ascended again disappointed, back into the darkening sky, and just as the Arctic fox scurried into action and up yet another incline in order to descend upon an unsuspecting lemming. The only sound made, as the lemming's life slowly ebbed away; its neck caught in the wide expectant mouth of this predator of the tundra, was the sound of the billowing chilly wind. Half a mile away, two Inuit men on a hunting trip were preparing themselves before what appeared to be a scuffed up pile of snow; they had to have had good experience to spot the hole in this weather. It was a breathing hole which a Ringed Seal had excavated in the ice for its own use. Both were clad in thick fur and sealskin and both had their hoods pulled up over their heads.

"How long do you think we will have to wait?" the smaller of the two men asked of the other. The bigger man was busy preparing a spear with which the both hoped to kill the ringed seal. He turned and smiled at the smaller man and then looked directly upward to catch a glimpse of some Arctic terns heading out towards the ice flow.

"Let us hope it is not too long! The weather is closing in, and they will all be waiting for us!"

As if in sympathy with the man's answer, a team of dogs that had been hauling their sled and tethered not a stone's throw away began to whimper and bark. The smaller man raised his hands to his mouth and let off a whistling sound, and they became instantly quiet. Now both men were prepared; the smaller Inuit man kneeling behind his bigger friend, who now had the spear held low above his shoulder ready to strike, appeared like icy statuesque sculptures. The seconds ticked by and the weather began to close in.

*****

Eleanor had gone to sleep early this evening having had an arduous time at the Oceanographic Institute. They had been allowed to continue with their work, but all shipping had been stopped from sailing with a national emergency being called, but everyone was aware that the prospect of nuclear holocaust was over. It wasn't long before she was in a deep and meaningful sleep, full of wonder, as she appeared to be swimming beneath the sea again but as a much smaller mammal. Without having to think, she blew bubbles up to the surface of her blowhole; Eleanor was in a vivid dream again and this time she was a Ringed Seal. Suddenly, bubbles appeared on the surface of the blowhole. Eleanor had put them there to trick any awaiting Polar Bears in to making a premature move; tension mounted. Below the ice and surface of the blowhole, Eleanor as a small species of seal with big bright eyes, and light coloured circular patterns on a darker grey back was veritably cavorting to and fro as if being instructed on nature's stage by the choreographer of a ballet, but she knew instinctively that she had been submerged for the maximum time she could spend underwater without taking breathe, and when feeding on Arctic cod at a depth of seventy metres, Eleanor decided to suddenly twist upward in a spiral movement to reach for what must have seemed the far distant light of her breathing hole. The arm which held the spear low over the larger Inuit man's right shoulder lifted slowly upwards to change its projected trajectory just like a piece of military ordnance readying itself. Then the arm struck and the commotion of the Ringed Seals death ended in seconds, but in a state of shock, Eleanor had awoken and drenched in sweat. All she could hear was the sound of what appeared to be the Shaman's voice; he was laughing. **"I told you, Eleanor, I would take you with me from time to time!"**

*****

Blood fused with water. Just as the light beyond the precipice of the hole had loomed, the seals expectancy had altered; before it had even surfaced it was shocked by a splash of water as the spear held by the larger man was launched from beyond the surface. The spear entered its cadaver and as rough hands gathered its being onto the ice; thick red blood ran into the snow. Within seconds the body was being skinned and the meat shredded into parcels which the smaller of the men wrapped up into bundles ready for transportation. As they worked, they recited a prayer to the spirit of the ringed seal. *"Oh spirit of the ringed seal, please forgive our intrusion, for we have to dine with our family, may you, oh spirit, go on your journey now!"* The dogs began to bark, howl and whimper again. Quickly the larger Inuit man stood up and threw pieces of the seal meat in the dog's direction which made the noise stop. It was right then, just as he fed the dogs; that he saw the **Raven** land. Standing in the snow, the man held his hand backwards as if to stop the smaller man from continuing his work; they both stood there and as a **'Purpley Blue-Black Raven'** with a crooked beak moved unafraid closer and closer towards them. The smaller man spoke first.

"What's the matter?"

The taller of the two men then went back to the carcass and retrieved some meat; he then threw it to the **Raven**. Unafraid, the **Raven** sidled right up to the meat and began feeding; the bird looked right up at him tilting its head from side to side again and again as if to get a panoramic view of its surroundings.

"It is Chulyin!" the taller man whispered to the other.

"Are you sure," the other man questioned.

"I am certain; look how brave he is; he has returned. Come, we better get back. He will be waiting for us when we arrive at the hut!"

*****

Four miles away from the ringed seal's blowhole and in blistering snowfall, the sled arrived at the hut. It took them no longer than half an hour to settle the dogs down and recover the seal meat for the great meeting. When the two men entered the hut, they were greeted by many others. Feathers danced up and down in front of their happy faces whilst drumbeats sounded.

"Chulyin is back," one of the throng shouted and they began to listen as he spoke.

"I was the Peregrine, Arctic Tern and the Raven', I flew upon the wind of time, and below the distant but pearlescent moon, and my dark silhouettes moved silently over the sunlit seas which licked like hungry brushes, at the night air, painting soft hues with the sunlight's condensate, touching and stroking and changing the palette of life. I was the Arctic Tern who sailed above the crests of wave after wave, and I watched all above and beneath as the God's swept the canvas of life with bursting light and all of the colours of the spectrum; magentas, indigos, violets, blues, greens, yellows and reds; all of which gently showed life, and all this was happening as mankind continued to try to emulate or conquer the designs of the Gods of nature, but none of man's invention can emulate the mother of pearl or coral of the deep and shallows which propel life into the great abyss, nor defeat a storm or swamping seas that vindicate the executive power of the Gods.

Come ye the moon,
Come ye the tide in temptation,
Come ye the corals sperm,
Go into the ocean's womb."

*****